Praise (some enhanced by Dinanukht) for
Exceptional Encounters:
Enhanced Reality Tales from Southeast Asia

"Paul Sochaczewski is a Literary Shaman. He writes otherworldly mantras, weaving intricate cloth with improbable yarns. He rummages inside your brain and then rearranges your reality with a deft twist, leaving you unsure about what is true and what is imagined. The hill tribe elders of northern Thailand know him as 'He Who Spins Clouds,' while in Guangdong, the children of Sea Gypsies call him, simply, 'The Navigator.' But we're not certain, for Sochaczewski is a literary joker. He's a smoker. A midnight toker. And he's playing his music in the sun."

—Gavin Gough, international travel photographer

"Another delightful literary roller-coaster ride from Paul Sochaczewski. He whirls us in his inimitable way, pausing to gaze at Southeast Asia's disappearing rainforests and threatened tribal peoples, while engagingly mixing fact and fiction to profile the movers, gods, con-men, and wannabe sultans who stride the netherworld between fact and fiction. A touch of George Orwell for our challenging times."

—Robin Hanbury-Tenison, explorer, author of
Finding Eden: A Journey into the Heart of Borneo

"These tales are unnervingly real to the reader familiar with Asia. Sochaczewski starts with germs of true events and factual issues, and elevates them into memorable folklore leavened with bursts of tongue-in-cheek satire. The tales are fiction, but illustrate the social, economic, and environmental realities that define Asia today."
—Anthony Sebastian, former international chairman, Forest Stewardship Council

"*Exceptional Encounters* explores a cast of upwardly mobile mystics, lawyers with tree spirits as clients, ambitious generals in need of pachyderm power, and canny female sultans living in a corner of the world we too often consider hard to figure out. Sochaczewski has lifted an Oz-like curtain on the 'factual' world of politics, business, and culture and given us insightful (and bitingly satirical) glimpses into a mischievous enhanced reality of Southeast Asia today."
—James Clad, author of *Behind the Myth: Business, Money & Power in Southeast Asia* and former US deputy assistant secretary of defense for Asia Pacific Affairs

"Storytelling alchemy. Sochaczewski starts with tales of memorable people and events, and creates soaring fiction that forces the reader to wonder where veracity ends and enhanced reality begins."
—Lesley S. Pullen, art historian at SOAS, University of London

"Paul Sochaczewski's marvelous Asian fantasies are firmly rooted in reality. His white elephant tale results from long-term study of these rare creatures. His Javanese "Mermaid Queen" evolves from his exploration of curious corners of Indonesia and extended contact with memorable sultans and rajahs. His vigilante army of orangutans is created from his scholarship and nature-blessed love for creatures large and small. *Exceptional Encounters* is one of those rare books where fact and fantasy first clash and then merge, ending with an explosively delightful vision of our fragile and poorly understood world."
—Harry Rolnick, author of *Spice Chronicles: Exotic Tales of a Hungry Traveler*

"At turns outrageous, hilarious, thoughtful, and darkly satirical. Once again, Sochaczewski has pushed the frontier of personal travel literature into a new dimension."

—Simon Lyster, chairman World Land Trust

"Here is Sochaczewski at his very best – *Exceptional Encounters* is sharp, witty, energetic, and unafraid to be irreverent. This book reminds me of the satire of *Catch-22* combined with the insightful travel memoirs of Bill Bryson and Mark Twain."

—Benedict Allen, BBC presenter, author of *Into the Crocodile's Nest: Journey Inside New Guinea* and *Hunting the Gugu: In Search of the Lost Ape-Men of Sumatra*

"With a wry eye and a mischievous sense of humor, in this highly entertaining collection Paul Sochaczewski smuggles literary contraband back and forth across the border between fact and fiction. Recalling the similarly genre-bending travel writing of Rory MacLean, there's a frisson in knowing that, in the topsy-turvy world of Southeast Asia, even the tallest of these tales could very easily be true."
—Tim Hannigan, author of *A Brief History of Indonesia* and *Raffles and the British Invasion of Java*

"Paul Sochaczewski is a writer's writer. For him writing is not work. It's living. It's smiling and laughing. You can hear him chuckling as he pecks at the keyboard. The man has some Mozart in him – he makes the world a better place."
—Jon Ferguson, author of *Jesus and Mary*

"Highly entertaining, contemporary, and original. Paul Sochaczewski's *Exceptional Encounters* is fiction, but truer than a lot of fact. It is written with a clarity and wry humor that greatly enables us to perceive, if not fully understand, 'mysterious Asia.' The supernaturalism of the East, which has long haunted the Western mind, so often evaporates under the scrutiny of direct observation – much like the particles of quantum mechanics. But here, through Sochaczewski's rich and distinctive style, the mysteries stand revealed, if not explained. Which is as it should be. Great fun."
—Lawrence Blair, author of *Rhythms of Vision: The Changing Patterns of Belief* and *Ring of Fire: An Indonesia Odyssey*

"The stories of *Exceptional Encounters* zither with wit and foamy erudition that delight and challenge in equal measure. They are fairyland castles raised up on a solid bedrock of deep, personal experience of Southeast Asia. Works of fantasy they may be, but they resonate scarily with the voice of prophecy, so that the riddle is not just how 'true' they are today but how 'true' they will prove tomorrow."
—Nigel Barley, author of *Snow Over Surabaya* and *Island of Demons*

"The tales in *Exceptional Encounters* reveal deep insights into the people and events of Southeast Asia, presented by an immensely talented and imaginative narrator."
—Jean-Noël Wetterwald, former director, United Nations High Commissioner of Refugees, author of *D'exils, d'espoirs et d'aventures: Un Suisse à la rencontre des réfugiés* and *Le Nouveau roi de Naples*

"*Exceptional Encounters* explores liminal warps – parallel universes in which the geopolitics, cultures, behaviors, and wisdoms of Southeast Asia are tossed, flipped, and transfigured for the reader's wonderment. As an added bonus, several of the book's fictional stories explore new ways by which we might better understand our eco-spirituality and relationship with nature."
—John Studley, author of *Hearing a Different Drummer: A New Paradigm for the "Keepers of the Forest"*

"This is travel writing evolved to a new dimension, full of wit, insight, and take-no-prisoner fabulations."
 —William Shakespeare, author of *Hamlet, Macbeth,* and *Titus Andronicus*

"The reader enters a rabbit hole with visions of Asia that are based on fact but seen through a brilliantly diffused looking-glass."
 —Alfred Russel Wallace, bug collector

"Too many big words and long sentences, and more humor than I usually tolerate. But Sochaczewski would make a worthy drinking companion on a hot rum-enhanced afternoon in Cuba. I've got tales. He's got tales. May the better writer win. But I've got bullfights and all he's got is mentally deranged orangutans. My round, I think."
 —Ernest Hemingway, author of *For Whom the Bell Tolls* and *The Old Man and the Sea*

"*Exceptional Encounters* rolls along like a runaway truck full of magic potions, scattering whimsy, acumen, and oft-hidden Asian truths along the way."
 —Somerset Maugham, author of *The Razor's Edge* and *Of Human Bondage*

"Full of wonderful stuff that I don't understand myself, but that other folks say is terrific. $S=EI^2$ where S is Sochaczewski, E is elegance, I is insight."
 —Albert Einstein, author of really important stuff

"What wonderful stories. Sex, violence, greed, ambition, and charisma. They remind me of me!"

—Sukarno, first president of Indonesia

"When the going gets weird, the weird read Paul Sochaczewski."

—Hunter S. Thompson, author of
Fear and Loathing in Las Vegas

"A collection of stories you can savor on many levels. The Asian storytelling of Somerset Maugham, the satire of Jonathan Swift, George Orwell, and Joseph Heller, the reality check of *Foreign Affairs*, and the dark humor of Roald Dahl."

—Valmiki, author of the *Ramayana*

Exceptional Encounters

Also by Paul Spencer Sochaczewski

An Inordinate Fondness for Beetles

Share Your Journey

Redheads

Distant Greens

The Sultan and the Mermaid Queen

The five-book *Curious Encounters of the Human Kind* series:
Myanmar (Burma)
Indonesia
Himalaya
Borneo
Southeast Asia

* * *

Co-authored with Jeffrey McNeely

Soul of the Tiger

Eco-Bluff Your Way to Instant Environmental Credibility

EXCEPTIONAL ENCOUNTERS

ENHANCED REALITY TALES FROM SOUTHEAST ASIA

PAUL SPENCER SOCHACZEWSKI

EXPLORER'S EYE PRESS

GENEVA, SWITZERLAND

ISBN: 978-2-940573-30-1

Cover photo courtesy of Dreamstime.
The image of the contemplative man is from *Der Wanderer über dem Nebelmeer* (*Wanderer Above the Sea of Fog*) by Caspar David Friedrich, c. 1818; public domain.

Book design by Stacey Aaronson

Published by:
Explorer's Eye Press
Geneva, Switzerland

This is a work of fiction. Any relation to real individuals, incidents, or locations is coincidental.

Printed in the United States of America

Dedicated to Dinanukht, the Mandaean god who
is half-man, half-book; he sits between the waters
of the worlds reading himself.

Dinanukht turns pages
Tales rumble in his stomach
Digests, then reflects

TABLE OF CONTENTS

Epilogue

Introduction
Whooshing Levitation
Explore enhanced reality.

I write about true unusual Asian encounters with exceptional people, of strange events that defy Western logic. Tales of folly and greed, ambition and dreams. My books (with the exception of my novel *Redheads*) are nonfiction – they tell of events that I experienced.

This book, however, takes the seeds of the true stories I've written earlier and applies the classic fiction writer's aerobic exercise by asking: *What if?* What if I were to take a germ of an idea, a pinch of veracity, and create, well, an untruth, but an untruth leaping off the ground, allowing the wind of levitation and bewilderment to whoosh through. But even soaring fiction needs to be anchored to the ground; we all know a kite won't fly without someone holding the string.

Kids, try this at home. Expand your world. Go beyond a slavish obligation to "tell the truth" and "get your facts right." Emulate a politician. Lie. But unlike a politician, as you gather by the campfire, tell whoppers that illustrate elusive truths. Fabulate. Imaginate. Explore enhanced reality.

PROLOGUE

Dinanukht Examines His Naval

Lint? Or letter?

Dinanukht's body is a book. He sits between the waters of the world, reading himself.

But, being a complex creature – god, sage, image, concept, will-of-the-wisp – Dinanukht ponders his "chicken or egg" dilemma.

Which came first, reading or writing?

This is a serious question for Dinanukht (who wants to be called Didi by his friends, but, being a bit of a curmudgeon has no close acquaintances).

Dinanukht reads voraciously, but not always with pleasure. He has persnickety tastes and finds he reads with greatest satisfaction works that he has written himself.

He sits between the waters of the world with the tools

of his trade. Next to him is a pot of indigo-colored ink, made by mixing crushed blueberries and unicorn blood. He wields a brush, made out of walrus whiskers, with the panache of Merlin casting a spell. He unrolls a length of parchment made from Cyclops fingernails that have been emulsified in Florida orange juice (with pulp), then pressed into paper-like form.

He squiggles. His squiggles are elegant and they flow like the finest Chinese calligraphy. A stroke down. A stroke across. He creates an L. He swirls and behold, he has created an O. Only a few more letters and he will have created LOVE. Or LOYALTY. Or LOTHARIO. He isn't sure yet.

In fact, he isn't sure about a lot of things. Like most serious readers, Dinanukht appreciates conundrums. Needs them, in fact.

For more weighty tomes he has set up an easel holding a chunk of flat basalt, with chisels and mallets. He repeats his labors on the rock with hammer and chisel. This time the letters are hard-edged, serious, with the weight of a Wagner opera that says "don't mess with me." L-O.

And all the while he thinks about language. At what point did a squiggle earn meaning in Language A, while remaining meaningless in Language B? You can't read without language. And you can't have written language without letters. Who comes up with this stuff?

"I think I will invent the next big invention in clothing," Dinanukht says to his friend Ariel. He is still learning his craft and doesn't have the advantage of an editor to simplify his sometimes clumsy word choice.

Ariel is attractive, and Dinanukht thinks all sorts of sweaty possibilities. But he knows he is not physically attractive. His body, after all, is a chunky book.

"Yes. My gift to personkind is this," he says, holding up a bright blue garment. "Something that will enable mortals to emulate me by reading themselves."

"And what might that be?" asks Ariel.

"Have a look. I have invented the Message T-Shirt."

And indeed he had.

Ariel slipped on the garment. She was a woman who looked good no matter what she wore.

Dinanukht looked on in pride. "Go ahead and read yourself," he said.

And she did. "Dinanukht went to the World of Light and all he got me was this lousy T-shirt."

Dinanukht smiled. "Think it'll fly?"

Exceptional Encounters

Cheng Ho Gardens

China reveals an imaginative new tactic in its takeover of the South China Sea.

NANYANG AUTONOMOUS REGION
China

"I'm going to show you our plans. I trust that you will be discrete with the information."

My host was Horace Wee, chief executive officer of Nanyang, the newest Special Administrative Region of China.

I was way out of my comfort zone.

Usually I seek out the curious, the esoteric, the eccentric quirks of life in Asia.

This time I was dining with the big boys.

Let's back up a few steps. While researching a story on China's role in the trade in tigers and snow leopards, I had met Hong Nei-yi, who is deputy minister of the Chinese equivalent of the attorney general's office. Hong told me what his office was doing to try to shut down the trade —

the laws they had passed, the beefing up of customs inspectors, the crackdown on traders, the educational campaigns aimed at consumers, the financial and technical support to the countries where tigers and snow leopards are found. And I sort of believed him, at least enough to write a balanced article for *The New York Times*.

Hong and his colleagues appreciated that, with my conservation background and loud mouth, I had given them a chance to explain their side of the story and had treated them fairly.

Now I was in Beijing trying to meet senior officials in the Ministry of Defense to attempt to understand the psychology of China's massive interventions in the South China Sea.

China is big. Seems silly to say that, but everything about the place is huge. Just off Tiananmen Square, one of the world's largest open urban areas, can be found government ministries that feature huge auditoriums, massive murals (romantic representations of the inherent goodness of the peasants is a common theme), and lots of meeting rooms where the chairs are covered with starched white cloth and green tea is poured in endless quantities. It was in such a meeting room that I met Horace Wee.

Wee offered me cookies, asked after my family, joked about English football (like me, he roots for Arsenal), made fun of Donald Trump, and told dirty jokes in quite good French. We bonded over our favorite Beatles songs. If he had been any friendlier I would have thought he was American. He is in his forties and speaks with an American accent, not surprising since he did his undergraduate degree in history at Princeton, then an MBA at Wharton, and worked with Microsoft for ten years and Boeing for three, soaking up the good vibes of Seattle.

"I'm going to the South China Sea tomorrow. You'll come with me."

It would have been churlish of me to refuse.

We flew in a military jet to the brand new military airport in the Spratly Islands, roughly equidistant from Ho Chi Minh City in Vietnam, the southern Philippines island of Palawan, and the Sultanate of Brunei on Borneo. The Spratly Island archipelago, claimed with varying degrees of vigor by Taiwan, Malaysia, the Philippines, and Vietnam, has been one of several South China Sea locations where China has waltzed in and colonized scattered small islands, considerably enhancing their real estate value by enlarging them through extensive land reclamation. Also, the Chinese have created dozens of new islands where previously there were only coral outcrops. This quiet takeover of a strategically and economically vital region has resulted in complaints, whining, and teeth-gnashing by Vietnam, Taiwan, Malaysia, Brunei, Indonesia, and the Philippines, all of which have various territorial claims. Mosquito bites on an elephant. The United States armed forces have rattled their sabers, but the Chinese smugly continue their grand engineering projects knowing that the Americans, for all their bluster and B-52s, aren't going to precipitate a shooting war.

The Chinese are creating a new form of empire building. Instead of marching into other people's territory and taking over, as did Napoleon, Hitler, and Genghis Khan, the Chinese are simply creating new territory (albeit on stretches of almost empty sea claimed by others). And by occupying these territories and creating infrastructure (and what is more infrastructural than a military base, or the world's gaudiest shopping mall, or a national tourism office?), other nations would have no choice but to acknowledge China's sovereignty. This tactic is "geopolitical genius," according to C.L. Ovis-James, a senior US diplomat with extensive Southeast Asian experience.

•••

We flew into the military airport in the center of the Spratly chain, using only a fraction of the three-thousand-meter-long runway. Horace Wee and I were billeted in the brand new Sheraton hotel, the first of what no doubt will be numerous joint projects. The hotel was not yet fully operational, but we settled in at the hotel's Nine-Dash-Line coffee shop for a bowl of quite good Penang laksa and Coke Zero with plenty of ice.

"Welcome to the future!" Wee said brightly.

"Nice hotel for a military base," I replied.

"We get a lot of high-level visitors from Beijing," Wee said. "They might be Communists, but even senior Party officials like a few comforts."

Nanyang, literally "southern ocean," is the term used to describe the geographical range of what are generally called Overseas Chinese, particularly those people living in the countries with competing claims to territory in the South China Sea. Put another way, the term describes China's demographic and financial influence in nearby countries in Southeast Asia. Some fourteen percent of Thais have Chinese blood, twenty-five percent of Malaysians, and seventy-four percent of Singaporeans. More to the point, throughout the region, and even in countries where there is a tiny Chinese minority (Vietnam, Indonesia, and the Philippines each have just one percent Chinese population), ethnic Chinese businessmen control the economy. One business journalist estimates that Overseas Chinese in Southeast Asia account for just three to four percent of the population but control about half the total regional economy and eighty-five percent of the financial industry. Overseas Chinese control business, they control natural resource extraction (which some people in the conservation world consider akin to rape and pillage) and, in many cases, control the government through spider-web-like business deals with powerful "indigenous" frontmen.

The South China Sea is hugely important. Some forty percent of China's oil imports pass through the sea, part of a $5 trillion annual seaborne trade. Militarily, the armed installations China has constructed provide de facto control of a vital region.

The step that logically follows de facto control, Wee implied, is absolute control. He then told me something simultaneously scary and brilliant.

"What I'm going to tell you is embargoed to tomorrow at 09.00 GMT."

I agreed.

"Not too far from here we are going to declare a new Special Administrative Region called Nanyang."

I was dumbfounded. "So you're creating a new territory that will have some flexibility in how they govern themselves, sort of like Hong Kong or Macau."

"Something like that."

"Why are you doing this?" I asked.

Wee didn't answer, at least not directly.

"We Chinese get a lot of bad press. We're not evil. We want to create a zone of capitalistic prosperity, open to everyone."

I must have looked befuddled.

So Wee, with admirable patience, explained the deal to me.

The island we were on, the one with the Sheraton and the runway considerably longer than the longest runway at

New York's JFK, with a harbor about the size of Rotterdam's, would remain a military base, as would the dozen or so other nearby islands created from sand dredged from the South China Sea. "Where we are now will be part of Yunnan Province."

That in itself was big news – the idea that China had formally incorporated what used to be the Spratly Islands into the mainstream of Chinese administration. This was a bigger story than Russia annexing Crimea. But it was done quietly, "a subtle conquest" one pundit calls it – a twenty-first-century land-grab without a shot being fired.

But then Wee got out some maps and architectural drawings.

"Look here." Wee pointed to a large chunk of the Archipelago Formerly Known as Spratly where work was underway on an enormous construction project consisting of the creation of some thirty new islands.

This impressive creation was called Nanyang.

Wee showed me the plan.

"See this large island? It doesn't exist yet!" he said proudly. His jabbed his finger at a circular blob of land roughly four times the size of Singapore. He explained that dredging had just begun to create this island from the shallow sea. It would be called Zhu Ying after a third-century Chinese explorer, and it would host an international airport with extensive facilities for private jets and helicopters. A modern harbor. Luxury hotels and casinos. A couple of golf courses and shopping malls that, Wee said, will make Dubai's shopping malls look like neighborhood strip malls. A lagoon for jet skiing and windsurfing. Theme parks from the major film studios. They're even creating an artificial coral reef to replace the natural one destroyed during construction. "It will be great for scuba diving, world class, better than Raja Empat or the Great Barrier Reef because we'll create mini super-bio-rich artificial reefs within the larger reef system," Wee said proudly.

"How will you do that?"

"We regularly confiscate enemy fishing boats and naval vessels which illegally enter our waters," Wee explained. "We clean out the fuel tanks – Nanyang will be highly eco-friendly – tow the vessels to the reef and sink them in twenty to thirty meters of water. To make it even more interesting, we're going to use state-of-the-art animatronics to populate the wrecks with giant squid, octopi, and sharks. We'll hold regular *son et lumière* shows – the first ever underwater. Regularly, we'll conceal treasure – gold coins, genuine Ming vases, Greek amphora – inside the wrecks so divers can go on modern-day treasure hunts. Fish and coral love shipwrecks. And people love to dive on them."

"Everything anyone could want for the holiday of a lifetime."

Wee ignored my sarcasm. "And residents of Nanyang can avoid the irritations of meddling American tax agents." Nanyang, he explained without using so many words, was also everything anyone could want for laundering money – it would be home to whatever financial institution wanted to open its doors, under Chinese monetary authority supervision, of course.

This was exciting and exhausting. But Wee wasn't finished.

"What's this area here on the map called Cheng Ho Gardens?" I asked.

"Ah, I'm really excited about this. I know good Party cadres shouldn't have big egos, but I'm very proud of this."

Cheng Ho Gardens, named after the famous Chinese Muslim eunuch admiral of the Ming Dynasty who explored much of the world in the fifteenth century, including Southeast Asia(it's a long story), was a combination retirement village, tax haven, and secure final living place for the world's rich, famous, and unloved.

Horace Wee put a humanitarian spin on Cheng Ho Gardens. "Throughout the world there are men and women who have served their countries but have nowhere to live after they retire. We're providing a place where they can own property, safely invest their savings, and build the homes of their dreams."

"Can't people do that anywhere?"

"Not the unfortunate people we're targeting. Think of nation builders – Ferdinand Marcos, Idi Amin, Jean-Bedel Bokassa, and Zia ul Haq. Inspirational leaders like Hosni Mubarak and Baby Doc. Freedom fighters Mobutu Sese Seko and Donald Rumsfeld, Joseph Kony and Charles Taylor. Augusto Pinochet. Muammar Gaddafi. Robert Mugabe. Bringers of development to primitive people such as Taib Mahmud and Najib Razak. Not to mention the entrepreneurs who deal in recreational chemicals – Pablo Escobar and Manuel Noriega. Socially conscious tycoons like

Donald Trump. Spiritual leaders like Jimmy Swaggart and Bhagwan Shree Rajneesh. The men and women who run multinational businesses that you Westerners sneer at and call evil – the Triads, the Cosa Nostra. Good, hard-working folks with families who have nowhere to go – when so-called 'civilized' countries refuse these kind people safe haven, they are denying good men and women their basic human rights. We're meeting a need the United Nations has ignored – safe haven for rich refugees. We hope to get the Nobel Peace Prize."

What Wee left unsaid (more Chinese genius) is this. China is desperate for rare earth minerals, timber, oil and natural gas, uranium, precious stones, medicinal plants, and body parts of endangered animals. Many of these treasures are found in countries that are poor, disorganized, and run by rabidly corrupt despots. China's main tactic has been (and no doubt will continue to be) to infiltrate such mineral-rich/ethics-poor countries by offering to build airports, dams, train lines, and roads in exchange for good terms on extraction rights.

But in addition to the airports and dams, which the dictator can point to proudly as examples of national development (and quietly pocket his ten percent commission), China offers these men (and a few women) a safe haven in Cheng Ho Gardens – a comfortable and secure refuge (with security guards trained by Israeli and Rhodesian consultants) in which to enjoy their golden years after the inevitable coup or downturn in business. "Win-win-win" as Wee explains.

With the panache of a huckster trying to sell time-shares in an Orlando condo ("just six miles from Disney World, and two golf courses nearby"), Horace Wee explained the procedure.

First, the prospective buyer makes a non-refundable deposit of ten million dollars for his Nanyang passport. I assume that this fee can be offset against normal cost-of-doing-business bribes the Chinese pay for permission to rape and pillage the buyer's country.

Then comes the fun part. The buyer can design his or her own island. Nothing off-the-shelf for these folks.

"One of our new citizens," Wee said, "from a wealthy East African country, wants an island in the shape of a male lion – the tail will be a links-style golf course, and the lion's mane will conceal hidden beaches with air-conditioned pavilions where he can relax with his wives – I think he has six, plus another few in training."

"Other designs are similarly intriguing?"

Wee went through some of the plans for the eighteen islands already committed. One North African gentleman wants his island to be in the shape of his jowly visage, so visitors flying in to Cheng Ho International Airport can be greeted by his smiling face. Another national opinion leader has commissioned Wee to build a tropical volcanic island, with a two-thousand-meter-tall volcano in the center.

"Which will erupt?"

"Not in the geological sense," Wee assured me. "But we will install a few things that he wants – a state-of-the-art pyrotechnics center within the volcano's cone, so the volcano will 'explode' fireworks on his birthday, and a roller coaster that will travel around and inside the volcano. He's going to call it the Vulcanoaster™."

"Nice name," I said.

"Yeah, my idea," Wee offered. "Please remember that we've registered the trademark, so make sure you put in the little 'TM' thingamajig."

Wee continued. "And there's a gentleman from a Slavic country who doesn't like sub-tropical weather, so we've created for him a series of gigantic terraces and mini-mountains. Thanks to the extensive solar energy system – after all, we aim for all of Nanyang to be 'green' and for residents of Cheng Ho Gardens to be good Earth citizens – each of the vast terraces will be air-conditioned, and the ground soil, shipped in from Canada, I think, will be lined with refrigeration pipes and underground irrigation systems. The idea is to create a series of temperate landscapes where his gardeners can grow apples, cherries, and roses. He'll have forests of maple, oak, and pine. In some areas he'll have snow for skiing and an ice rink where he can play hockey and his young figure skating girlfriends can spend their free time. We'll introduce Northern Hemisphere animals so he'll feel at home – foxes, rabbits, and moose. His main house will be in the form of a Bavarian hunting lodge. Very tasteful."

I was impressed. But a bit apprehensive. Wee was revealing too much.

"Why are you telling me all this? Surely not to get publicity in the *Times*."

"Let's grab a beer and I'll answer your question."

We shifted a short distance to the Nanyang Sheraton's Peranakan-themed "Becak Bar."

"I enjoyed your articles about Savantis," Wee said.

"You read those?" Wee was referring to the pieces I wrote years ago about a new country that was being planned by the reconstituted Knights Templar.

I had replied to a tiny classified ad in the *International Herald Tribune* that had offered "an economically available, State Sanctioned Hereditary Knighthood."

Some wannabe nobles had resurrected the Knights Templar, a prominent and powerful group of medieval Christian noblemen who protected pilgrims on the crusader routes to Jerusalem.

A group of mostly British visionaries recreated the Ancient and Noble Order of Knights Templar as a non-profit organization legally based in Israel. For just a single $5,000 fee, and fees of $500 year (less than my golf club fees), I could be honored in an investiture involving apanages and escutcheons. I'd get to wear a special ring and have use of two castles and the opportunity to buy privately bottled Knights Templar Bordeaux.

And even better, the title came with citizenship of a new country they're creating, code-named Savantis.

"Only five people know where it is," said Knights Templar Chancellor Savant Graham Renshaw-Heron. But from reading between the lines, I figured they were buying an island in the Philippines or the Caribbean. According to Sir Graham, the thousand or so "locals" were enthusiastic about becoming Savantists and living under five dukes who would control the country. The nation would become a beacon of hearty, mostly British-bred, capitalistic enthusiasm, with economic benefits accruing from the planned casinos, resorts, golf courses, offshore banking, and flags of convenience shipping. Sort of like Nanyang.

Savantis, Sir Graham assured me, was "just an inch away from receiving United Nations recognition."

"I've read most of the things you've written," Wee continued. "As I recall, you didn't accept the invitation Sir Graham offered to join the Knights Templar and become a citizen of Savantis."

"They weren't terribly serious," I said.

"No, and you're a serious guy."

I had a feeling what was coming next.

"I'll cut to the chase. I'd like to offer you a job. It comes with a Nanyang passport. I'll give you a long-stay suite in one of the new hotels being built in Cheng Ho Gardens — you can choose the Ritz-Carlton or Four Seasons or Aman. Full membership in the golf club. Annual salary of, say, half a million. Of course that's tax-free and concealed from prying eyes."

"That's very generous. But to do what?"

"Be our director of communications. Not everyone in the outside world understands our humanitarian vision, our commitment to nature conservation, our intent to develop and showcase the most innovative architectural designs. You understand our positioning. You are a friend of the new, improved, user-friendly China. People trust you."

"Surely you, or one of your colleagues, could do that," I said.

"Technically, perhaps. But look at us. We're Chinese — physically and culturally. People wouldn't believe our sincerity. But you're from New York. Everybody trusts New Yorkers."

"Does it come with a title?" I asked.

"Like I said, director of communications."

I made a face.

"Or if you prefer, we could call you senior vice president of truth and media impact. How about that?"

"I was actually thinking of some kind of royal title, you know, like a knighthood."

It was Wee's turn to make a face. "Impossible my friend. We haven't had royalty since the Ching Dynasty. Nanyang might have some, er, unusual laws, but it's still part of the People's Republic of China. One for all and all for one."

"Pity, I've always wanted to be called the Prince Formerly Known as Artist."

We talked for a while and I said I'd let him know.

Which I did, a few days later. I told Wee my journalistic ethics wouldn't allow me to "switch sides." That I didn't particularly like the idea of living on an isolated island. That I couldn't abandon my roots.

Wee understood and promised we could remain friends. "I'll invite you to the opening of the hotel complex," he said. "I'll introduce you to Paris Hilton and Justin Bieber and Kim Kardashian."

The White Rajah of Borneo Returns

British playboy claims his title and
restores historic harem.

MALUKA JAYA
Kalimantan, Indonesia

he White Rajah had returned.

There was hardly a murmur from the populace — neither gratitude nor fear, neither protest nor curiosity. Life went on.

The White Rajah was born a commoner, Alexander Mustafa Luce. At the age of thirty-three he changed his name by deed poll to Rajah Alexander Hare II in memory of his early nineteenth-century ancestor Alexander Hare — slave owner, harem builder, and the first white rajah of Borneo.

Rajah Alexander Hare II (né Luce) had been visiting the Indonesian Borneo coastal city of Banjarmasin for years, first as a curious tourist researching his ancestor's history, then as a business partner of Sultan Ibrahim bin Harrods, with whom he had invested in a series of increasingly lucrative real estate ventures domiciled in the Channel Islands. Hare II had made the sultan a rich man. But Hare II didn't take out his share of the profits – he put them into a trust account run by the sultan's brother, a risky strategy considering the number of foreigners who have been ripped off by Asian rulers.

But it paid off. Win-win. The sultan wanted cash safely stored in European banks. Hare II wanted land and permission to recreate the kingdom he thought was rightfully his birthright.

Those are the bare bones of the story. But to understand the rest of the Hare II saga, I visited Maluka Jaya during the early days of his reign and met the White Rajah and some of his women. I could only have had this access because I had befriended Sultan Ibrahim some years earlier, helping him prepare his bid to buy Crystal Palace Football Club in London. Shortly after my visit (I doubt there is a correlation), Hare II decided that Maluka Jaya was off limits to journalists; the information I publish here was obtained through interviews with Hare's women, vague hearsay, and imaginings.

* * *

A twenty-first-century sultan, even one as well-placed and rich as Ibrahim bin Harrods, doesn't have the ultimate power his ancestors had to simply give a foreigner land. Indonesia today is a republic, and most of the more than three hundred royal families in the country have no civil power. Except in this case Sultan Ibrahim *did* hold a government position – the wise voters of South Kalimantan province had elected him governor.

So Hare II and Sultan Ibrahim made a deal. The sultan, in his capacity as governor, would lease a large tract of land in the swampy coastal zone south of Banjarmasin to Hare II, who would develop it, according to zoning permits on public record, as a multi-use site comprising an industrial park, a private nature reserve, and an exclusive management training campus for young Indonesian entrepreneurs. Hare II paid a nominal rent along with the electricity, water, and taxes. His contract stipulated that he would share profits with the province of South Kalimantan.

And Sultan Ibrahim, using his sovereign powers, gave Hare II a royal title in recognition of his "services to the Sultanate of Banjarmasin." Hare II interpreted this as a knighthood (after all, the ceremony included the Sultan blessing him with sacred royal sword), and added "Sir" to his business card.

This would have hardly been worth writing about had it not been for Hare II's inclination to follow in the footsteps and bedroom antics of his ancestor.

First, a quick quiz for students of Asian history. Who was the first White Rajah of Borneo?

No points if you answered James Brooke, the Englishman who was appointed Rajah of Sarawak in 1841 by the

Sultan of Brunei and who started a three-rajah reign that lasted until 1946.

The first White Rajah of Borneo was the Englishman Alexander Hare, who had his moment in the Borneo sun some thirty years before James Brooke.

Hare left behind no monuments, no lasting social innovations, no glittering palaces. He was not a patron of the arts, nor was he keen on landscaped gardens. What he did leave were hundreds of illegitimate children and many thousands of miserable slaves.

Alexander Hare (1775–1834) was an English merchant who joined a trading company in Portugal around 1800, then moved to Calcutta several years later where, according to legend, he promptly set up housekeeping with a fourteen-year-old dancing girl named Dishta.

He later settled in the Malaysian port of Malacca, where he met Stamford Raffles, the Lieutenant-Governor of British Java (sorry, this gets confusing; the Malaysian city of Malacca has no relation to Hare's territory of Maluka in Borneo — which is sometimes written Moluko, Molucco, Molukko, or Maloekoe – or to the far eastern Indonesian Molucca Islands, also known as the Moluccas or Maluku). Hare had already exhibited his proclivity for young women, and Raffles's biographer Tim Hannigan says that in Malacca, Hare ran "a highly irregular household with barely post-pubescent Asian women of various races tumbling out of every bedroom."

Hare was sent to Borneo in 1812 by Raffles to become Political Commissioner of the Government for the Native States in Borneo, and resident of Banjarmasin.

During the 1811–1816 British Interregnum, when England took temporary control over Java from the Dutch (who were busy losing battles closer to home against Napoleon), Raffles responded to a request from Sultan Sulaiman al-Mutamidullah of Banjar for help in suppressing lawlessness and piracy (similar to the reasons the Sultan of Brunei sought the assistance of James Brooke some three decades later). Raffles saw the opportunity to establish an exclusive trading relationship – timber, gold, and diamonds among the most valuable commodities – with Banjarmasin, located on the southern tip of the island of Borneo, and appointed Hare to establish the bond.

The sultan welcomed the economic benefits and military protection such a treaty with Britain would provide, and he gave Hare a chunk of swampy, unproductive land six times the size of Singapore.

It was hardly a salubrious base, but Hare wasn't picky. He set himself up as ruler of a personal kingdom called Maluka, issuing his own coinage and indulging in a personal business that was illegal in British-controlled Indonesia: slavery.

He also indulged in his predilection: young women. Lots and lots of young women.

Shortly after Hare arrived in Banjarmasin, he immediately broke East India Company policy and Raffles's own regulations for British residents at native courts. A resident was not supposed to accept any kind of gift from a king, including gifts of land. (Perhaps trying to distance himself from Hare, Sultan Sulaiman later complained that

Hare's land was meant to be used for his private residence, and was not intended to house unruly convicts who frightened the local citizens.)

And the women running around servicing Hare, well, that just wasn't the way British colonial officials were expected to behave.

According to the few historians who bother to study him, Alexander Hare was either a talented diplomat who secured a strategic treaty with an important sultan, or an egocentric, law-breaking wastrel who used his position to assuage his own needs.

In his reports Raffles praised Alexander Hare, saying that under his administration, Banjarmasin had been "reduced to order and regulation." Raffles effused that Hare was "a gentleman whose desire after useful knowledge and whose zealous exertions in the cause he has undertaken, are perhaps unrivaled."

Not so, according to Tim Hannigan, author of *Raffles and the British Invasion of Java*: "The truth was that under Hare, Banjarmasin was reduced to poverty, disorder, and unprofitability."

The British managers reported that Hare "had been received at the Sultan's Court with the most particular respect and attention, and had been hailed throughout his Highness's [George III] dominions as the deliverer of that once powerful Kingdom.

Not true, according to historian Graham Irwin, who

wrote that Hare was "plausible, unscrupulous, and ambitious [and whose] desire was to found a kingdom of his own where he could luxuriate in oriental splendour surrounded by slaves and ladies of the harem."

But Raffles defended Hare, noting that the strategy to engage the sultan had been Hare's and there was not "any other person competent from local knowledge or respectability of character to whom the charge could have been entrusted."

Was appointing Hare a brilliant tactic or something Raffles would privately regret?

The general consensus is that appointing Hare was one of Raffles's least successful management decisions. According to Hannigan, Hare was guilty of "unhinged despotism, flagrant disregard for British colonial law, and outright sexual excess."

Alexander Hare's legacy led to two phrases that are jolly sound bites in British colonial history. Hare's blatant extravagances, oversized testosterone surge, and outrageous chutzpah led to a colonial embarrassment known interchangeably, as the Banjarmasin Enormity and the Banjarmasin Outrage.

What did Hare do to deserve such vitriol?

He engaged in the slave trade. He did not pay any duty on his own trade and was accused of using the salt monopoly for his own profit. He charged the running costs of his shaggy kingdom to the British crown. And then there were the girls. Oh my.

Alexander Hare's kingdom was located an hour's easy drive south of Banjarmasin, a rambling city of some six hundred thousand in southern Kalimantan. It was here that Hare II chose to replicate his ancestor's kingdom.

With two friends, relatives of Sultan Ibrahim of Banjarmasin, I drove along a good two-lane road. It is a flat, featureless region of floodplains and muddy rivers, just a step up from a swampy morass, with rice paddies, rubber gardens, and large blockish houses designed to attract swiftlets whose saliva-constructed nests are the key ingredient in bird's-nest soup. Here and there we passed the on-road commerce that one finds throughout Indonesia — motorcycle dealers, small restaurants offering duck rice, a few shops, not much of anything. And, like elsewhere in Indonesia, motorcyclists with the road sense of gerbils weaved in and out of the sparse traffic, spewing litter in their wake.

On a tidal inlet we found the village of Maluka, the namesake hamlet of Hare's scruffy empire. This is where Hare II decided to rebuild his ancestor's kingdom, which he named Maluka Jaya (Victorious Maluka).

Hare II started modestly. One wife and three domestic helpers from East Java.

And the slave trade? "No such thing," he told me.

Just the opposite, in fact. Hare ran a center for battered women, women who had been trafficked, women who had nowhere else to go. In exchange for sisterhood and a clean, safe place to live, they tended Hare II's organic guava and pineapple orchards, his goats, his free-range chickens. And, according to *sotto voce* reports, they also tended to Hare's personal needs.

According to most accounts, some five years after starting Maluka Jaya, the number of women in Hare II's community had increased to sixty. Some were young, others old. Some were disabled. Some slim and dark-skinned, others plump and fair. All worked. He provided medical care and education and helped the women become self-sufficient and proud of themselves. He encouraged physical fitness and good nutrition. Some women learned yoga, others meditation. Yet others mastered a form of Indonesian martial arts called *silat*.

In return they were intensely loyal to Hare II.

And he was an easy man for the women to be devoted to – tall, thin, muscular (he wasn't afraid of outdoor work), and with a soft, yet knowing voice that one community member described as "hypnotic." Hare II wasn't a cruel man. He was ambitious, imaginative, courageous and, we must not forget, highly sexual.

It's hardly worth saying, but sex is a complex thing. It's physical and spiritual, it's pleasure and pain, it's control and submissiveness, guile and honesty.

It's dangerous to psychoanalyze Hare II's need for sex and control. Was it an enhanced libido and an addiction to physical pleasure? Was it a need to dominate? An overly controlling mother or a mother who had neglected him? A deep-seated drive to be as curious a historical character as his ancestor Hare I?

And what of his women? His harem, if that is the correct term, participated voluntarily. In many ways they held the power over him. Not quite like Amazons or the Sirens of Greek legend, not really like the *dakinis* of Tantric Buddhism, the women we call Hare II's harem could just as easily be labeled as Hare II's controllers in the sense that they controlled *his* life. He couldn't live without them – a fact of life they understood fully but were too smart to mention.

Media reports have said that Hare II was running a mind-control cult, sort of like James Jones did at Jonestown, and that he used a combination of brainwashing and intimidation to get his women to tend his fields and satisfy his manly desires. Some people say he cleverly manipulated the women by bringing in clergymen to explain how Hare II was the long-awaited prophet, and salvation could only come through following his orders and meeting his needs. Some people say he engaged black magic shamans to put spells on the women.

I saw none of this during my short visit. But, as I said, that visit took place at the beginning of his "reign."

No doubt the "sorority sister effect" also played a role – the women were part of a community, and there was strong pressure on each person not to rock the boat or question the rules.

It's possible that Hare obtained their loyalty simply by

force of charisma. He respected the women of his extended family, paid them, and made them feel worthy, conditions that rarely existed for women in mainstream Indonesian society.

The women were not forced to stay or work. He paid allowances to their families back in the village, sent their children (who sometimes were his) to school, and protected them from local thugs. He might have even put a spell on them – hypnotism had been mentioned, or love charms – but regardless of his tactics, his community of women grew and flourished. If some of them chose to share his air-conditioned bedroom, that was their choice.

His women called him "Sir Rajah Alex."

And, perhaps most surprisingly, none of them gave away any secrets or had a bad word to say. Although the women, who called themselves FSR (short for Femmes de Sir Rajah), regularly visited the city of Banjarmasin – even though they dealt with traders and outside workers, even though they returned to their home villages to visit their families – no FSR ever spoke ill of Hare. Just the opposite. On the few occasions he was mentioned in a conversation, the women would smile, say "he's a good man," and shut up. Hare had achieved the unimaginable – he developed a group of Indonesian women who didn't gossip.

Then the idyll was broken when a group of local thugs stormed into Maluka Jaya.

According to urban legends, and recountings by a

handful of Hare's women (I don't know what to call them – lovers? employees? shareholders? slaves?) who witnessed the events, three men arrived on motorcycles at Hare II's estate late one October afternoon. They paused at the organic farm a few hundred meters from the Big House, where Hare II lived and kept his office. They raped two of the women working in the fields, while a third woman escaped and cried for help. The men, armed with handguns and Javanese ceremonial daggers called *keris*, then drove to the Big House, stormed in, and confronted Hare II, who was at his desk having a Skype conversation with a business colleague in Hong Kong.

"These men rushed in and threatened Sir Rajah Alex," one witness, who asked not to be identified, said. "They were loud and drunk and very frightening. They didn't even take off their shoes, which bothered us because Sir Rajah Alex always stressed the importance of good manners."

The men confronted Hare II and, in a combination of Bahasa Indonesia and broken English, told him to give them the papers to his estate and all his money and computers. They also asked where he kept the whiskey.

By this time all the women who were within earshot had rushed into the office. So had Hare II's three beagles, named Ping, Pang, and Pong. His two cats, Panca and Sila, had quickly scampered the other way once the confrontation began.

Without hesitation, the women surrounded the thugs. When the ruffians threatened them with guns, the dogs nipped at the men's ankles and the women swarmed on the invaders like fire ants on a wounded caterpillar. "This is for raping our sisters," they cried with each blow. "And this is for threatening Sir Rajah Alex."

Soon the fight was over. Two of the thugs were dead, the third had broken ribs, a battered face, and severe groin injuries due to repeated kicks to his genital region.

—•••—

Indonesian justice is a bit better today than in the past few decades, and that posed a problem for Hare and his women. Should they trust the police? Should they trust the judges and the legal system? If they called the police would the women get a fair hearing? Or were there Big Man forces behind the thugs who could alter the course of justice? Could they successfully bribe the judges? Would a police investigation bring unwanted publicity to Maluka Jaya? Could Hare II's friend the sultan/governor intervene on their behalf?

Perhaps, some of the women argued, the good citizens of Maluka Jaya were operating under a higher order of justice. After all, Hare II was like an adopted son to the Sultan of Banjarmasin, which made him a prince, not to mention a knight. And Hare himself was a rajah, with all that implied in terms of close relationships with the gods.

What would you have done?

Hare II left the decision to his women.

They dismantled the thugs's motorcycles (although there was vigorous internal debate about this, since motorcycles were quite useful and these were bright red and blue and almost new) and put the parts into old oil drums.

They stuffed the two dead men into other old oil drums, then rolled the drums to the Maluku Jaya fishing boat moored just meters away. On the high tide they motored out to sea and, after adding rocks and chains to increase the weight, they sealed the barrels (but cut some holes to allow water to enter, thereby ensuring they would sink) and tossed them overboard at a deep oceanic trench two hours from shore.

And the poor chap who survived? It's not clear (things rarely are in Indonesia) but I understand that Maya, the head shaman of Maluka Jaya, put a spell on the man, inserting needles in his lungs and filling his brain with mystical gibberish so powerful that he became a gurgling idiot. The FSR drove him some eight hours into the rainforest north of Banjarmasin and let him loose. He was found two days later by a group of Dayak farmers, starving, dying of thirst, and babbling about *pontianak* ghosts with long teeth and stringy hair. The Dayaks were convinced he was a demon, a ghost, a whatever, and wanted nothing to do with him. They gave him some water and dried meat and left him where they had found him. None of their clan ever returned to that location, but the story of the deranged, almost naked, man is still told around campfires in Dayak villages.

And then it was quiet again at Maluka Jaya.

When rumors about a "troublesome event" at Maluka Jaya reached Jakarta, I sought out Ms. H, the lady who had been my first informant when I started writing about Hare II's kingdom. Once employed as Hare II's chief accountant and senior masseuse, she now worked as a public relations director for a major automobile company in Jakarta, and volunteered as a guide at the National Museum. In her spare time she played violin in the Jakarta Symphony.

Ms. H heard, through her friends who remained at Maluka Jaya, that following the rape and murder, Hare II went into a "dark depression." He was distraught that he hadn't protected the two FSR who were raped, and he was afraid that the story would leak out and he would lose his kingdom. With Hare II spending most of his time in bed (alone, Ms. H. added), a power struggle began among the more ambitious FSRs, and things started to fall apart. I checked around, and some of the people Hare II was usually in touch with — business contacts, old friends, even the sultan himself — confirmed they hadn't heard from him for months. "It's as if he was sucked down into the muddy tidal flats of Maluka Jaya," one of Hare II's friends said.

SLOUCHING TOWARD BETHLEHEM

Can a top-secret CIA plan mobilize guerrilla orangutans to save Borneo's rainforest?

OTAK PUSING NATIONAL PARK
Kalimantan, Indonesia

 was not allowed to tell this story. I was sworn to secrecy. But after many years, and with the protagonists likely dead, this story has leaked. Most of the newspaper reports have been inaccurate. The truth needs to be told.

The story involves rogue CIA agents, brain-modified orangutans, wealthy do-gooding conservationists, angry tribal people of the rainforest, corrupt government officials, and Chinese infiltration. Oh yes, global warming and Victor Frankenstein-like experiments. What could possibly go wrong?

Here's the problem. In spite of public commitments, in spite of economic boycotts, in spite of almost daily leaks about corruption on a vast scale, the leaders of Indonesia and Malaysia have not stopped the destruction of their tropical forests on the island of Borneo, a gigantic land mass they share (with the Sultanate of Brunei, which has good conservation practices). At international conferences the power brokers make encouraging statements about protecting the homelands of indigenous people and maintaining their countries' biodiversity. Once the meetings are over they return home and work with middlemen who blithely cut the largest trees for valuable hardwood, then denude the land and plant oil palm – vast, endless, monoculture oil palm plantations that are a virtual desert for wildlife and people.

And that led impassioned conservationist – former-US senator, former-senior CIA official – Joe Lawrence to come up with a solution. Engage wild orangutans to act as a vigilante force to stop the destruction.

Throughout the world, indigenous people and conservationists have tried various tactics to stop rainforest destruction. Protests. Scientific studies declaring an area "a global biodiversity hotspot." Reader-friendly feature articles focusing on endangered charismatic megavertebrates, as well as on quirky lesser-known critters like the Jesus Christ lizard of Central America (it walks on water) or the naked mole rat of East Africa (famous for being a hairless cold-blooded mammal with walrus-like teeth, able to survive oxygen deprivation and having natural resistance to cancer). Appeals to the global community. Legal battles.

Impassioned pleas to "save our forests." Inviting an influx of foreign researchers. Ditto for foreign eco-tourists. Increasingly, frustrated indigenous people have turned to violence. There isn't a trick in the book that hasn't been tried.

In Sarawak, one of two Malaysian states on Borneo, a Swiss man named Bruno Manser lived with a band of semi-nomadic tribal Penans for four years and encouraged them to erect and man symbolic blockades of timber roads and activities. For his part, Manser engaged the complementary tactics of generating international public and governmental support.

It worked at first. Timber operators grudgingly respected the blockades, partly because they were wary of media attention, partly because the blockades had been blessed by tribal shamans who threatened that *really bad* things would happen to anyone who broke the barriers.

And then the blockades stopped working. The timber operators and oil palm plantation developers said, *cukup,* that's enough, and the police started to arrest blockaders, allowing the oil palm bosses to go about their business.

Joe Lawrence was angry about global destruction of nature, he was smart, and he had oodles of money, mainly from a legacy left by his father, Hubert Lawrence. Perhaps it was guilt that drove Joe Lawrence, since his father's money had been earned in the agro-chemical industry.

Perhaps Joe was simply a good person. Perhaps he was mad, a modern-day Don Quixote out to right wrongs. Joe's likely dead now, so we'll never know what really drove him.

Joe was also the younger brother of Rod Lawrence, the one-time head of the INF, the International Nature Federation, at one time the world's largest and most powerful nature conservation group. Tutored by his brother, Joe understood the workings of the conservation movement, and perhaps was frustrated by the inability of the well-intentioned environmental NGOs to accomplish any real results.

Joe Lawrence was, like his brother Rod, a United States senator. Whereas Rod was elected to represent Rhode Island, Joe was elected in neighboring Massachusetts. He had a rapid Congressional career, rising to the head of the Senate Intelligence Committee, and then, after losing a close election to a new-generation Kennedy, working as deputy director of the CIA. He had friends in strategic places.

Joe Lawrence was also the paramour of Beatrix Beverly Derek (called B.B. by all), one-time head of communications for the INF, who had developed a fondness for orangutans when she went to Borneo to report on conservation efforts (and where she was almost sexually assaulted by a randy adolescent orangutan named Ringo).

Oh yes, one more thing. Joe was a genius. His talent, exhibited by earning PhDs from MIT and Imperial College, London, was the ability to create techniques to manipulate behavior through brain implants and cognitive pharmacology.

He was a scientific virtuoso, and his friends were similarly gifted.

This was never going to be easy.

I ran into Joe Lawrence by accident while wandering around the park headquarters of Otak Pusing National Park, in the Indonesian province of South Kalimantan. The vast protected area was one of the largest tracts of mostly intact rainforest in Borneo and home to a large wild orangutan population. It was also a dumping ground for young orangutans that had been captured (usually by killing their mothers), sold throughout Asia as pets, and then rescued and sent to Otak Pusing's rehabilitation center to learn how to survive in the wild. However, because they grew up almost as members of human families, many of these rehabilitant animals weren't sure whether they were ape or human, and this caused psychological and behavioral problems.

One steamy afternoon I was eating lunch with some of the park guards, a simple and unappetizing meal of rice and boiled river fish. I mentioned that I had seen a white man roaming around earlier. He didn't look like a tourist and I asked who he was.

"That's Mister Joe," one guy said.

"And what does he do?"

They weren't sure. They said he was *kaya*, rich, had lots of fancy gear, never spoke with the lowly park guards but always huddled with Pak Adam, the haughty national park director. He had his own support staff and was going upriver later that day.

So I wandered around and found Joe checking his equipment. I introduced myself and he was polite, but obviously wary.

He wouldn't answer my direct questions. I explained I was a writer and producer for BBC and had been writing about conservation in Indonesia for many years. It hadn't hurt that I had written a sympathetic biography of Bruno Manser (the best book about him, but that's my opinion) and that I had been imprisoned in Kuching, Sarawak's capital, for refusing to reveal my sources in an article I wrote about corruption in the state. Then B.B. Derek, his partner in this escapade, whispered something to Joe. They excused themselves for a while and returned. The gist of the conversation, I speculate, was that B.B. had told Joe that it would be good to have a responsible journalist document the operation. Joe had evidently disagreed and politely told me that our meeting was over. An hour later I heard his speedboat heading up a small tributary.

I thought I would never see Joe again.

But I kept on asking about him from folks involved in conservation in the States. And I returned several times to Otak Pusing, as part of a major story (and hopefully a book) I was writing about collusion between the army, police, government ministers, and big business to deprive poor local people of their human and environmental rights. Secrets don't stay secret very long in Asia. My friends the guards were helpful and they fed me bits of information.

I'm being self-serving here. I also returned regularly to Otak Pusing National Park because it's a nice place, and I adore watching orangutans. It's a good excuse to get out of the office.

The rumors from the guards were increasingly tantalizing. Some people who looked like scientists had visited Mister Joe and gone upriver with him in boats filled with *matériel*. A major construction was taking place in an isolated corner of the park; it was called Camp Hutan Jaya. The local laborers who worked there were sworn to secrecy, which meant nothing, of course. My friends the national park guards had been told by their boss, Pak Adam, not to venture too close.

So I took the only logical course of action. On a subsequent visit to Otak Pusing a year after I had first briefly met Joe Lawrence, I bribed three national park guards to take me to Joe's camp. Poor guys, their pay is miserable. We cooked up a cover story for our arrival that timber operators and poachers had been spotted in the neighborhood. The tip-off had come from a reliable source and we had come to investigate. Had Joe seen anything suspicious?

The journey up winding black-water rivers took three hours. Joe wasn't happy to see us, but he was quite un-American in his diplomatic skills (meaning he was quiet and civil) and in his Asian-like ability to hide his emotions. Since I was a white man, and therefore de facto head of the invading force, Joe and B.B. invited me to lunch.

The meal was fried rice, ferns fried with wild garlic,

and a bland river fish soup made palatable only by the addition of a big dollop of fermented prawn paste. Sweat beads formed on Joe's bald pate. B.B.'s frizzy hair glowed reddish-brown when it caught a ray of sunlight coming through the window.

"So, this is Camp Hutan Jaya," I said in a neutral tone. I stopped talking, waiting for them to fill in the silence.

No reply.

"So, what are you doing here?" I then asked, forcing myself to pretend to enjoy the food.

They looked at each other. "Just field research. Bryophytes and flying squirrels. Catching a few butterflies," Joe finally said.

I didn't respond and forced myself to eat a few more mouthfuls. I had a few Snickers in my backpack so I would be okay if I wanted a snack later.

We talked about conservation. Our conversation confirmed what sources in the States had told me – Joe and B.B. *really* cared about the fate of Borneo's forests and the people and wildlife therein. Sure, some people are cynical about the motives of a couple of rich foreigners working to protect a Third World resource, but I think their hearts were in the right place.

"Nothing has worked," Joe said, some passion in his voice. "Protests haven't worked. Blockades haven't worked. International pressure, financial sanctions, legal cases. Nothing has worked."

"Nothing has worked." It became his mantra, as if the three-word slogan had become a Biblical injunction, like "go forth and multiply." His use of the phrase reminded me how the three-word chant has become the go-to form of mass communication: "Let's go, Mets," in sports. "I'll be back," "Hasta la vista, baby," and "Shaken, not stirred" in films. "Burn, baby! Burn!" and "We Shall Overcome" in the tense 1960s, "Yes we can," and "Four more years" in happier political times, and "Drain the swamp," "Build that wall," and "Lock her up" in more recent discourse.

But what was he actually doing in his remote corner of an isolated lowland rainforest?

I asked for a tour of the camp.

I had intuited their goal — to protect the rainforest — but I didn't learn their game plan; Joe and B.B. didn't give me the modus operandi during that first visit to their camp. I asked probing questions, but Joe and B.B. refused to get drawn in. This was their world and I was an intruder. An unappetizing lunch was all they were going to offer.

Nevertheless, my friends the guards had succeeded where I had failed. While I was eating bony fish and getting stonewalled by Joe and B.B., my pals had hunkered down with the laborers working at Camp Hutan Jaya and heard stories that sounded like *Back to the Future* meets *Dog Whisperer* meets *MacGyver* meets *Doctor Who* meets *Mission Impossible* (yes, they get American TV shows and films in Borneo). The guards had learned that Joe and B.B. were training young rehabilitant orangutans. To what purpose wasn't clear. The foreign scientists at the camp were hard-working and had lots of high-tech equipment at their disposal. It was all secretive, and therefore exciting, and therefore ripe for speculation.

The national park guards and I returned to park headquarters right after lunch.

I would have to wait a couple of years to learn exactly what Joe and B.B. had in mind. I must say, it was worth the wait.

I was frustrated being so close to a big story. But I couldn't write anything based solely on rumors that a mad scientist was on a mad quest. Well, I suppose I *could* have written a colorful feature that combined an allusion to Kurtz from *Heart of Darkness* with a "whatever happened to that bright young politician?" slant. But I never got around to writing it. First, I didn't have the facts. And I got distracted by other things (I had all of Southeast Asia on which to report and there was no shortage of corruption, nature destruction, idiot drivers, crooked monks, spiritual scams, modern-day slavery, and human trafficking to write about.).

—•••—

Meanwhile, the tribal protests continued, the timber operators continued to rape and pillage the forest, and the population of wild orangutans continued to shrink.

Then, two years after my lunch with Joe and B.B., I

was visiting an isolated Kenyah longhouse near Gunung Malu National Park, on the other side of Borneo from Otak Pusing. There I heard strange tales about the creatures the longhouse folks called *"wali mias,"* meaning "guardian orangutans," that were attacking timber workers who were cutting large rainforest trees. The timber workers who were attacked by the mysterious orangutans, my longhouse friends said, had a more sinister term for the animals, *"setan mias"* meaning "demon orangutan." It seemed that rogue orangutan vigilantes were protecting the rainforest.

And then I heard similar stories from longhouse friends in other areas who also were living near forests that big shots wanted to convert into oil palm plantations. *Wali mias. Setan mias.* It's all in your point of view.

And then the stories told around the campfires about orangutans kidnapping timber workers became hard international news. I didn't break the story; that was Jon Goh, of the *Sacramento Bee.*

NEAR GUNUNG MALU NATIONAL PARK, Borneo
Special to the *Sacramento Bee*
by Jonathan Goh

A "ghost" ape has been terrorizing laborers in
timber operations in this isolated corner of Borneo.
According to exclusive interviews with villagers
and timber camp employees in the vicinity of Gunung
Malu National Park, a UNESCO World Heritage Site and

one of the most biologically diverse rainforests in the world, "giant ape-like creatures" have been kidnapping timber cutters, carrying them off into the deep forest, and abandoning the frightened captives, who were left on their own to attempt to return to either a settlement or their base camp.

"It looked like King Kong. It was at least two meters tall. Maybe three," said Ibrahim, one of the abducted chain saw operators. "I was minding my own business, getting ready to start cutting a tree, and 'whoosh,' next thing I knew this demon had me on his shoulder and was running into the forest as fast as a clouded leopard. I'm lucky to be alive."

Ibrahim, like other abductees, have refused to return to work.

These tales have caused a panic among the timber operators who now find it difficult to find staff to cut the trees.

Tree felling, accompanied by selling valuable (and often protected) tropical hardwoods, is the first step in a process of deforestation that has changed the landscape of much of Borneo. Once a forest has been cleared, the denuded land is planted with oil palm trees.

"I think there's something in the water that these boys are drinking," said Jong Kim-song, field director of the Hong Nei-yi Timber Enterprise, one of the affected companies that has temporarily stopped operations. Mr. Jong, who has not visited the deep-forest site of the abductions, said confidently that "this is a temporary set-back. In this day and age we certainly don't believe in giant ape ghosts. We'll be back in business very soon."

Harry Kallang, a Kenyah tribal villager in Rumah Sehat longhouse in another part of Borneo, noted that he's heard similar stories about abductions of timber operatives in the forests near his community. "Before the *wali mias* came, we heard chain saws each day," Kallang said. "We were really angry, because this is tribal land. Now the timber cutting has stopped. For the moment we are happy. . . ."

It was a story I couldn't ignore any longer.

———◆◆◆———

I returned to Otak Pusing National Park and asked the guards to take me back to Mister Joe's Camp Hutan Jaya.

The camp had grown to eight wooden, tin-roofed buildings.

Joe had aged. He was still tall and thin, but his hair was now more gray than brown, and he had grown a beard, giving him a vaguely Abraham Lincoln look. B.B. looked pretty much the same as before — not too tall, a bit over-weight, taken to wearing tank tops that showed off her best feature — her substantial breasts. They were so prominent, in fact, that my national park guard friends were certain that her initials referred to "Big Boobs."

They invited me to dinner and offered me accommodation for the night.

Before the visit I had done some homework, triggered by the longhouse stories and Jon Goh's article.

I suspected, but had no proof, that Joe and B.B. had created a deliberately complex network of NGOs in the United States, Indonesia, and Malaysia that they quietly funded and even more quietly managed. Through these money-laundering NGOs (you'd recognize their names), they had tried to arm the indigenous tribes of Borneo's rainforests to engage in a guerrilla war against the people Joe and B.B. called "the devil's pillagers." This tactic, of course, has been a staple of American foreign policy for centuries. Sort of like Ronald Reagan's arming of the Contras in Nicaragua. When I was at World Wildlife Fund in the 1980s we used a similar, but less violent tactic. We at WWF positioned ourselves as the "good guys" – we wore nice clothes, wrote scientific reports about how the world was being destroyed, and were willing to discuss things rationally with people we disliked. We quietly funded Greenpeace to play "bad cop" ("our Cubans," we called them) to create an uproar so that we could play "good cop" and walk into the boardroom and tell the whaling nations or the industrial polluters, "You've got a problem, folks. Maybe we can help resolve it." That tactic worked in the 1980s, but since then Greenpeace started to use science and wash regularly while WWF became so corporate that they were more comfortable working as an arm of industry rather than as a fighting, testosterone-laden, principle-led NGO.

———•••———

But I digress. (See how powerful a three-word phrase can be? I think I'll use this device more often. And you should use it in your writing as well. In fact there are two ways to harness the power of three. The first is in the Triple Whammy, where the reader is calmed by the elegance of a three-step concept. Consider "snap, crackle, and pop." "Life, liberty, and the pursuit of happiness." "Veni, vidi, vici." The second is the "Two Refusals Before Yes" writing rule that no problem should be immediately solved; it's best to first have a defeat. Then a second setback. And only on the third attempt can you have a "yes." Look for it in action movies; it even works for romantic comedies.)

Enough digression.

———•◆•———

"Tell me what you're really doing here," I said during the dinner. Joe and B.B. had obviously changed the camp cook since my first meal with them; we ate a decent chicken curry served with bamboo shoots steamed with ginger.

As they drank with pleasure the Australian Shiraz I had brought, they spouted false generalities. Field research. Smithsonian grant. Work on their graduate degrees – they said they had returned to university as "mature students."

"Listen," I said in my best reporter voice. "There has been a spate of attacks on people working for timber companies and oil palm plantations." (I love speaking with intelligent people with whom I can use words like "spate.") "The attacks were sometimes gentle, sometimes violent.

It's all very hush-hush, but the word around the long-houses is that the aggressors are 'demon orangutans.'"

I pulled out a print of Jon Goh's article and placed it on the table.

Joe glanced at it. "And your point is?"

"My sources tell me it's your operation." Maybe Joe and B.B. realized I was bluffing, perhaps not. "My theory, which I'm going to publish if you don't give me the details, is that you're involved in a highly secretive, highly illegal, probably unethical, scientifically advanced plan to train wild orangutans to kidnap the people who are destroying the forest. I'm not quite sure how you did it, but I have enough for a good story."

Joe took a chicken bone from his mouth and placed it carefully next to his plate, as if he was removing an opponent's pawn from a chess board. "We need to talk."

I already knew part of what Joe told me, but I let him ramble. All the tribal people of Borneo were angry at the destruction of the forest and the arrogance of the people in high places who treated the rural folks as second-class citizens. The people most directly affected – the Penans of Sarawak – were never fighters, and their culture didn't encourage them to become overly aggressive. But their cousins belonging to other indigenous groups – the Kayans, Kenyahs, Kelabits, Muruts, and particularly the Ibans – *are* aggressive when pushed into a corner, and in some areas they reverted to the head-hunting tactics of their ancestors.

However, this type of revolt was quickly extinguished by the Malaysian and Indonesian police forces who punished entire communities for the deeds of a few hotheads. The indigenous guerrillas were crushed.

"Nothing was working," Joe said.

"And then Joe had his big idea," added B.B.

Instead of arming the people of the rainforest, they decided to arm the animals.

"But of course you can't teach an orangutan to use a *parang* or a shotgun," Joe said, while B.B. nodded.

"But they're amazingly strong creatures," B.B. said, always ready to complete Joe's thoughts.

I recalled how B.B. was almost savaged by a horny adolescent male orangutan. First-hand knowledge.

"And they're smart," Joe said. "So, voilà."

"And what exactly was this voilà moment?" I asked.

Joe and B.B. smiled at each other. "Should we tell him?" Joe asked.

———◆———

We were all up at dawn, as most serious people are in the tropics. I met the senior team. They told me their first names, not their family names. I didn't push. Men and women, about seven of them. Mostly youngish. Casual. A couple of older military types, maybe ex-Marines. A mix of Americans and Europeans. Plus a Chinese woman, a Japanese guy. No Indonesians or Malaysians. Maybe it was a question of security, or maybe the locals didn't have the appropriate technical skills.

There was a small house for Joe and B.B; a comfortable dormitory for the professionals; a less comfortable dormitory for the local staff; a machine shop for the maintenance of outboard engines, boats, solar panels, and generators; a dining hall and kitchen; a lab; a clinic that served animals and people; and a building that doubled as a library and rec hall (table tennis seemed to be a more attractive pastime than reading). Each building was air-conditioned, the grounds were swept and tidy, and the staff wore casual clothes but were clean and neat. Almost a military operation.

Most interesting, and a touch otherworldly, was to find a series of modern laboratories in the middle of the Borneo rainforest. I don't know much about scientific equipment, but it seemed like they had good stuff, and lots of it. Machines that looked like a sophisticated drug lab. Oscilloscopes and a machine shop, lasers and a clinic, X-ray machines, an MRI tunnel, and a CAT-scan machine. There was a huge satellite dish on the roof. I envied them – perhaps they even received baseball games.

"We were curious whether we could train orangutans to 'own the fight,'" Joe said as he showed me around.

I was beginning to tire of his three-word calls to action, but I let him continue.

The biggest challenge, it seemed, was in disciplining an animal that behaved like (and with the intelligence and attention span of) a four-year-old child.

"We tried everything," B.B. said. Cognitive reinforcement. Rewards and punishment. Hypnosis."

"You hypnotized orangutans?"

"We're not sure. They're really spacey animals and it was hard to tell whether they had gone under or not."

"Finally," Joe said, "we found something that worked."

———•••———

Otak Pusing National Park occupies a vast area, about the size of the American state of Connecticut. It's filled with blackwater rivers, lots of primary lowland rainforest, and a large population of rehabilitant orangutans. These are animals that, in most cases, had been captured as infants when someone shot their mothers. This used to be a common occurrence when orangutans were sold to the pet trade, but when that market mostly dried up (score one for enforcement of laws), the adult animals were still in danger because they were shot when they wandered into oil palm plantations for an easy meal. In some cases the surviving youngsters were raised by humans and weren't entirely sure whether they were *Pongo pygmaeus* or *Homo sapiens*. The place is full of young apes that are habituated to people and like to hang around the feeding platforms where they enjoy free lunches.

The objective, not always realized, of the "rehabilitation" centers is to teach the captive orangutans survival skills so they can be transferred back into the wild and live like, well, wild orangutans.

But Joe and B.B. wanted to flip this idea. Instead of teaching orangutans to become independent of people and return to the forest, Joe and B.B. wanted to ensure that the apes were completely programmed to enact behaviors instilled by human training, drugs, and manipulation. Psy-ops for apes. They called it Operation Slouch, in reference to the "rough beast" in Yeats's poem "The Second Coming." The orangutans became the Stepford Wives of the animal kingdom. Not quite robots, certainly not like humans. Apes with a purpose.

"Here's Buster," B.B. said, introducing me to a small orangutan. Buster climbed into my arms and began playing with the hair on my chest.

Here I must digress again. Having up close and personal contact with an orangutan is one of life's greatest thrills. It's more intense than the relationship you might have with a dog, for instance. Orangutans are curious, mischievous, and strong. And their russet-colored hair reminds me of a Tuscan sunset.

"Come along, Buster," B.B. said, taking his hand and leading him to an open-air shed. "Time for school"

Joe and B.B., of course, weren't the first people to acknowledge and ponder the intelligence of orangutans.

In the Malaysian state of Sabah, on the northern corner of Borneo, I looked into the eyes of a rehabilitant male orangutan named Bee Jay (I was trying, unsuccessfully, to teach him to write his name) and was reminded of a comment made by Malcolm MacDonald, former governor-general of colonial Malaya and Borneo: "These members of the order Primates contemplate you, when you meet them, with melancholy eyes, as if they had just read Darwin's *Origin of Species* and were painfully aware of being your poor relations who have not done so well in life."

But do we over-anthropomorphize them? Are they aware? Can they cogitate? Can they truly learn a human language? Are they mindful of the implications of their actions?

Carl Linnaeus, the Swedish scientist who developed the modern scheme of binomial nomenclature, the system used for modern taxonomy, said, "It is remarkable that the stupidest ape differs so little from the wisest man, that the surveyor of nature has yet to be found who can draw the line between them."

Sue Savage-Rumbaugh, who has studied the intelligence of a number of ape species, argues that the orangutans' human-like emotions, intellect, and ability to acquire language should make them eligible for "semi-human" legal status. She is convinced that orangutans are at least "morally equivalent" to profoundly mentally challenged children. "We certainly would not put these children in a zoo to be gawked at as examples of nature," she says, "nor would we permit medical experimentation to be conducted on them."

In 2014 an Argentine court supported this view when it ruled in favor of a habeas corpus petition filed on behalf of Sandra, a twenty-nine-year-old Sumatran orangutan that had spent the previous twenty years in captivity at the

Buenos Aires zoo. The petition, filed by the Association of Professional Lawyers for Animal Rights, cited "the unjustified confinement of an animal with probable cognitive capability." The court ruled that an orangutan is a "non-human person" and has some of the same legal rights as a human; she should not be treated as an object. Call it legal semantics if you will, but the court considered Sandra as a human in a philosophical sense, rather than physical, and she was transferred to a less confining primate sanctuary in Brazil.

And orangutans can be aggressive, a trait Joe and B.B. were keen to make use of.

Biruté Galdikas is a pioneer of orangutan rehabilitation efforts and has worked for four decades in Tanjung Puting National Park in Indonesian Kalimantan – she has been tireless in her efforts to stop poaching and protect the rainforest. In her *National Geographic* articles, she recounts tales of life at her Camp Leakey in Kalimantan. She tells of schizophrenic orangutans that jump the animal/human line all the time. They murder. They rape. They steal. They vandalize. They refuse to pay attention in class. They put dirty things in their mouths. They beg. They act like people.

As B.B. knew, male orangutans have been known to sexually assault women. Syarif Kassim Alkadrie, the second Sultan of Pontianak in southern Borneo, who ruled from 1808–1819, told J. Burn, an English visitor, that an orangutan had carried off one of his female slaves. The animal kept the woman prisoner for some fourteen months, but she later escaped. When the Sultan sensed that Burn was skeptical, Burn replied that he believed the story, since he had heard from others that such kidnappings were common in the region. And a story with better credibility: Galdikas tells of how Gondul, a rehabilitant orangutan she had raised from infancy (for a while Gondul slept with Biruté Galdikas and her husband Rod Brindamour), grabbed the cook, ripped off her sarong, and tried to rape her.

For a cinematographic parallel, one might look at the closing sequence in Bo Derek's 1981 film *Tarzan the Ape Man* (in which an orangutan found only in Malaysia and Indonesia features in a movie allegedly set in Africa and shot in Sri Lanka). Actress Bo Derek came dangerously close to being sexually assaulted by the orangutan. When Miles O'Keeffe, her leading man, was tossed aside by the enamored, seemingly tame, ape. *Playboy* magazine, in a picture spread showing the incident, noted that during a love scene: "C.J., the jealous orangutan, didn't much like the idea of Tarzan and Jane having fun without him. In a totally impromptu move, he pulled 195-pound [88-kilogram] Miles O'Keeffe off Bo, interrupting one of the movie's steamier scenes ... 'We wrestled with him for an hour and a half,' recalled Derek. 'Orangutans are several times stronger than people and have four things to grab you with.'"

These incidents have both a biological and a psychocultural origin. Wild adolescent male orangutans are like their testosterone-infused human cousins – eager for sex, any time, any place. The trouble is that the adult females in a given territory are jealously protected by the alpha males, the critters with the distinctive throat pouches. And the females don't want to have anything to do with the younger males – the future of their offspring relies, they unconsciously realize, by producing babies fathered by the strongest dominant males. So the adolescent males act like the Donald Trumps of the rainforest – they spot an unprotected female, move in quickly, assault her, and then scamper off to eat some wild figs.

So a quick "grab and run" is hard-wired into adolescent male orangutans.

—◆◆◆—

The big question for Joe and B.B. was how could they train orangutans to move toward the noise of chain saws and trucks, pick out individuals cutting trees, carry them off into the forest, and then release them, unharmed.

Like George Harrison's song, the answer didn't come easy.

Joe and B.B. had initially hoped that the orangutans would respond to mind-control training.

In a human context this is often called brainwashing and is a literary device much loved by writers of spy novels.

In *The Manchurian Candidate*, Richard Condon describes how a group of soldiers, captured in Korea during the Korean War, were manipulated:

The principles of excitation, as outlined by Pavlov in 1894, are immutable and apply to every psychological problem no matter how remote it may appear at first. Conditioned reflexes do not involve volitional thinking. Words produce associative reflexes. "Splendid," "Marvelous," and "magnificent" give us an unconscious lift because we have been conditioned to that feeling in them. The words "hot," "boiling," and "steam" have a warm quality because of their associativity.

Inflection and gesture have been conditioned as intensifiers of word conditionings, as Andrew Salter, the Pavlovian disciple, writes.

Salter shows that when one sees the essence of the unconscious mind to be conditioning, one is in a strategic position to develop a sound understanding of the deepest wellsprings of human behavior. Conditioning is based upon associative reflexes that use words or symbols as triggers of installed automatic reactions. Conditioning, called brainwashing by the news agencies, is the production of reactions in the human organism through the use of associative reflexes.

So that's the first problem that Joe and B.B. had to face. Humans come with built-in emotional reactions to certain words (a tactic perhaps used consciously by Donald Trump during the 2016 election campaign when he described a variety of goals as "huge," "stupendous," "wonderful," and "amazing," and finished off such an announcement with trust-building seal-the-deal phrases like "Believe me.")

But orangutans obviously don't have a language that humans can access; the word "splendid" means as much to them, at least initially, as "awful." But they do react to tone of voice and body language cues, and they certainly can be taught, like dogs, to associate certain words with desired actions. On a simpler level this is what Pavlov did in his experiments when he taught dogs to salivate at the sound of a bell.

Lawrence's team experimented with simple "brain-washing." In *The Manchurian Candidate* the main character, Shaw, has been given certain cues to further modify his behavior, such as when he is instructed to play solitaire, he subconsciously understands that he must do so, and when the Queen of Diamonds turns up, he must wait patiently for a forthcoming order.

Joe and B.B. never managed to train orangutans with this technique and instead chose high-tech embellishments – brain implants to stimulate pain and pleasure centers, drugs, and practical training.

———•••———

Some years later I tracked down some of the folks involved in the project to try to understand how the orangutans were trained as forest guerillas. They spoke in frustrating generalities and revealed no clear procedure; many steps in the training process remained mysteries, like reading a recipe for baking an elaborate cake that omits many of the ingredients and gives no indication of quantities, baking time, and other useful tips.

One major challenge was to determine how "human-like" the animals' learning curve would be.

Orangutan brain physiology is similar to that of humans. Orangutans are among our closest relatives; we share some 97% of our DNA with the red apes (compared to 99% of shared DNA with chimpanzees). One widely publicized (and widely debated) study pointed out that physical similarities might be more important than DNA matches in determining which of the great apes are our closest relatives, since humans share at least twenty-eight unique physical characteristics with orangutans but only two with chimps and seven with gorillas. And another analysis indicates that an adult human has some sixteen billion neurons in the cerebral cortex, compared to 6.2 billion for chimpanzees, 8.9 billion for orangutans, and 9.1 billion for gorillas.

Everyone who works with orangutans knows they are patient and able to solve mechanical problems — they are good at picking locks and escaping from cages, for example. They easily learn to mimic human behavior — in captivity they might brush their teeth or eat with a spoon. Like human children they are tactile, adorable, and enjoy human company. It's impossible to be in the company of rehabilitant orangutans without feeling both empathy and affection.

A study of six populations of orangutans in Sumatra and Borneo identified twenty-four behaviors that show evidence of being culturally transmitted; many of the behaviors involve tool use – using sticks to dig seeds out of fruit or to poke into tree holes to obtain insects, or using leaves as gloves to protect against spiny fruit.

But it is misleading to think that an orangutan's intelligence equates with a human being's. Orangutans are animals that use their intelligence to find food – they have good memories for remembering which trees might be fruiting and where they are located. They are clever, even intelligent by our standards. But they are not people.

And while many attempts have been made to teach American Sign Language to orangutans (as has also been attempted with chimpanzees and gorillas), it is unclear just how much real communication has been achieved by these long-term experiments. And since orangutans lack the vocal cords necessary for human-like speech, it's unlikely we will ever achieve the holy grail of having a sensible conversation with an orangutan; up to now we can only communicate by interpreting each other's actions.

Orangutans are animals, and regardless of how clever they are, Joe's trainers quickly found that it was wrong to assume they had a human's power to reason or realize how their actions might fit into a bigger picture – in this case protection of the forest.

Nevertheless, a training protocol did evolve.

The young orangutans, which had either entered the rehabilitation program as infants or had been born in the controlled environment of the rehabilitation center, were placed in a group with a human teacher. Women turned out to be better educators than men and were dubbed "Guerrilla Girls."

The animals went through an intensive and lengthy boot camp involving stimulus-response, reward-punishment training. This included "old school" methods such as the techniques used to train guard dogs and circus animals. Additionally, remote-controlled electrodes were inserted in the orangutans' brains, primarily in the nucleus accumbens. These electrodes were placed in the animal's pleasure and pain centers to generate excitory and inhibitory responses to encourage the ape to perform desired actions.

And simultaneously the orangutans underwent what one person described as "bionic enhancement." A GPS tracker was inserted into the gluteus maximus muscle; Camp Hutan Jaya scientists called this a "Butt Compass." Additionally, a tiny video cam was inserted into the shoulder, and a miniaturized speaker was inserted into the ear canal to enable the animal's handler to send verbal instructions. Besides being minute, they also have state-of-the-art batteries, like those in heart pacemakers but considerably more powerful, and with much longer lives. These devices are top-secret CIA inventions, having been field tested on ISIS prisoners of war held at secure interrogation sites in Egypt and Jordan.

As part of the reward/punishment training, subjects were taught to move quietly through the forest, cautiously approach the sound of chain saws and motor vehicles, identify a "target individual" (usually a man with a chain saw), "kidnap" the target, and abscond with the target in spite of his vocal and physical protestations.

The animals were simultaneously taught to respond to verbal commands (transmitted by the trainers via the ear canal speaker inserted earlier) such as "capture," "carry," "north/south/east/west," "abandon," and "flee." As the animal became proficient, the trainers would link these commands with reward/punishment brain stimuli through the remote-controlled electrodes.

Continually, the apes also underwent a rigorous process of real-life simulations, similar to the techniques used to train guide dogs or guard dogs.

Additionally, and perhaps not surprising given Joe's background, the guerrilla orangutans were given cocktails of intelligence-enhancing and hypnotic drugs. This concoction, code-named by Joe and B.B. as CPH5, in reference to CPH4, the drug manufactured in Luc Besson's film *Lucy*, includes varying dosages of dopamine, serotonin, methylphenidate, amphetamines, and neuro-enhancers. The professional staff, whom I suspected occasionally sampled the concoction themselves, usually referred to the drug cocktail as Perky Pongo. The intention was to stimulate the nucleus accumbens of the brain to facilitate positive motivation and reward.

Then it was time for graduation. The trained animals,

called Slouchers, were helicoptered to various parts of Borneo where timber operations were taking place. Their remote human handlers, working from on-ground intelligence, stolen operational maps from timber companies, and satellite surveillance, directed the Slouchers toward timber camps, forest-cutting sites, and palm oil plantations. The Slouchers were then triggered to perform the task for which they had been trained. A Sloucher would quietly approach a man with a chain saw, quickly embrace him in a bear hug ("PPE, or primate-primate-embrace" in Joe's parlance), and swiftly move away from the other humans toward the deep forest. After traveling several kilometers, the orangutan guerrilla would then release the frightened man who would be left to his own devices to find his way home. If he made it to safety, he would have a strange and terrifying tale to tell his superstitious work colleagues. The orangutan guerrilla, no doubt soiled by the captive man peeing his pants, would calmly climb up into the trees and quickly leave the scene, free to find a female in heat to pass the time while awaiting another assignment in days or weeks to come.

—◆—

It was a long night. Softened by the Shiraz (we went through two bottles), we chatted freely and sort of began to like each other. I brought out a bottle of seventeen-year-old Wild Turkey and a few joints (good stuff, grown by the bored national park guards). We were halfway through the bourbon when I popped the big question: "What's the CIA's interest in all this?"

"To save the rainforest." Emphatic. End of sentence.

"You were with the CIA. Maybe still are. What's the *real* reason?"

"I told you," Joe said with a bit of annoyance. Rainforest destruction exacerbates climate change, so we're helping maintain the planet for future generations."

I like a guy who can use a word like exacerbate. "And the *real* reason?" I asked.

"The CIA is very eco-conscious. Climate change. Species loss. Things like that."

"And the *real* reason?"

"No, truly, the American intelligence network is genuinely interested in protecting the environment."

A few drinks and lots of tokes later I rephrased the question. "Wow, that's great the CIA cares about tarsiers and centipedes and hornbills."

"What the fuck are you talking about?" Joe said.

"Let's drink to the CIA and its environmental consciousness," I added.

"Ooh, cynicism," B.B. said in a soft voice. "Sexy."

"Regime change, okay?" Joe said with finality. "Pass that joint will you?"

B.B. was giving me "the look" that said either "be careful," or "I don't trust you," or "yes, you're on to something." A tough woman to read.

"Change the Ree-Jeem," Joe chanted. "French for Louis *quatorze.*"

"Marie Antoinette was brought down by the CIA, you know," added B.B.

"Then a toast to dear departed misunderstood headless Marie."

"And Marie's ghost is walking around the rainforest as we speak?" I conjectured.

"Create enough instability to bring down the governments and pave the way for our own hand-selected guys to flourish. Like flowers," Joe said with a giggle. "From the Portuguese. Or Latin. F-L-O-W-E-R-ish. Blooms in Borneo. Remove the bad guys. Once our guys get in, we pack up shop. Shut the shop." Even stoned, Joe couldn't stop speaking in his three-word phrases. But B.B. and I joined in and chanted. "Shut the shop. Shut the shop."

By this time B.B. was caressing my leg underneath the table with her foot. I left her and Joe to finish the bottle and staggered off to my simple camp bed in the dormitory used by the researchers.

———•••———

I lost touch with Joe and B.B. for a while, but I heard stories that things had turned bad.

The original goal of the Slouchers capturing a chain saw operator and carrying him a few kilometers into the forest to dump him there was only one part of the equation. If the captured laborer found his way back to the timber camp, it was believed he would be so frightened and hallucinatory from lack of water and food that he would babble about a giant demon orangutan. Soon, no workers would venture into the forest.

But some Slouchers went off-*piste*.

No one knew precisely what had gone wrong. Everyone had a theory but the only sure thing was that some orangutan guerrillas had gone rogue, in spite of their training, in spite of the sophisticated medical and technical implants, in spite of their supervision by controllers in Camp Hutan Jaya.

Maybe, as they became older, the orangutans overrode the controls and became *too* aggressive, *too* protective of their territories. When a rogue orangutan guerrilla picked up a chain saw operator, he might bite the man on the shoulder or face, or try to tear his arm off. Yes, the orangutan would carry the man many kilometers into the forest, but instead of releasing him unharmed, he would climb a tree and throw the man to the ground like a sack of potatoes. In short, the animals went from being guardians to killers.

In at least one case, the orangutans became *too* smart, and realized that the *real bad* human demons weren't the men who wielded the chain saws or those who drove the trucks. The bigger devils were the better-dressed men, the alpha males, who didn't get their hands too dirty, who shouted orders, who sometimes never ventured into the forest but stayed safely in the simple, but better-protected timber camp and rural offices of oil palm developers.

This happened one evening, just at dusk, as Jong Kim-song, the timber company official mentioned in

Jonathan Goh's article, was returning to his cabin after playing in a football scrimmage with other camp employees. It was the only time Jong evidenced a touch of democratic inclination, and the laborers enjoyed their perceived permission to tackle him hard and kick away at his shins and calves and elbow him when he went up for a header. But Jong was Korean, and he knew he had to maintain a tough posture. He put up with the bruises and gave as many as he got.

That evening at sundown, as Jong approached his cabin, it started to rain. He was only about fifty meters from his destination when he was grabbed by a large male orangutan and quickly whisked into the surrounding forest. No one heard his screams, which were drowned out by the thunderstorm. Days later his mangled body was found a kilometer from the timber camp. Jong's corpse was decapitated and his head, chewed or pulled off – it was hard to tell – was found thirty meters away. No one was certain, but it looked like the head had been kicked several times.

<hr>

Over time the judgement of some Slouchers became warped. For some animals the border between "good" and "bad" victims became blurred. Maybe the errant Slouchers had brain freezes and lost the ability to tell a bad guy from a good guy. Reports filtered out about orangutans attacking innocent farmers who were clearing small patches of land near their longhouses. Some orangutans even abducted village women working in the fields.

Nevertheless, some of the Slouchers performed as expected and are still roaming the forests of Borneo looking for bad guys. I thought of Charles Bronson in *Death Wish*, or Clint Eastwood in *Dirty Harry*. If orangutans could speak, would they say "Make my day"?

----•••----

It's now some ten years after Operation Slouch stopped activities and "shut the shop."

The results were mixed. For a while timber operations virtually stopped. Then the timber companies started to send armed guards into the forest to protect the workers. During the course of one abduction, an orangutan guerrilla was shot and killed. His body was brought back to the timber camp where it was dissected and the implants were found. Local security agencies, with the help of Chinese spy agencies that were eager to help, learned to override the remote commands coming from Camp Hutan Jaya and instructed the orangutans to roam deep into the forest and attack other orangutans instead of people.

Operation Slouch did achieve one of its goals, however. It created regime change. Unfortunately for the CIA the regime changed into a series of even more corrupt, dictator-driven, forest-destroying, Chinese-sympathizing oligarchies that are still in place.

----•••----

And Joe and B.B.?

They haven't been heard from for years.

I went to Camp Hutan Jaya and found a large patch of secondary forest had grown over the site of their camp. Digging through the underbrush, I saw charred remains of the camp buildings. No sign of Joe and B.B. or their staff.

It is rumored that once the Chinese figured out how to override the system, they turned some of the Slouchers against their makers. And (remember, this is rumor), by this time Joe and B.B. were alone in Camp Hutan Jaya; their foreign colleagues had all departed. My theory: One morning during a training session, Joe and B.B. were savaged and killed by two of their young trainee orangutans (perhaps controlled remotely by Chinese technicians). The private Camp Hutan Jaya security guys wrapped the bodies in burlap bags filled with stones and dropped the corpses into a river several kilometers from Camp Hutan Jaya. They then burned the remainder of the camp and sold some of the electronic equipment on the black market.

———•••———

Yet, years later, in the longhouses of Borneo, I still occasionally hear campfire tales of giant, killer orangutans. Some stories say that females have learned the aggressive behavior and are teaching it to their offspring. The commonly heard hope of the village folks is that the rogue orangutans are smart enough to differentiate between the good guys and the bad guys.

The Sultana's Education

How Java's controversial female ruler grew into the job.

PARANGKUSOMO and YOGYAKARTA

Indonesia

ecent news stories from Central Java, Indonesia:

Incident I:

The Sultan of Yogyakarta, Hamengkubuwono X, announced that his heir to the most powerful royal dynasty in Indonesia would be the eldest of his five daughters, whom he designated as Pembayun, or Crown Princess. The sultan's decision generated widespread condemnation from his subjects and brothers who argued that only a man was competent to handle this important position.

Incident II:

Yogyakarta police noted in recent months an uptick in difficult-to-explain deaths. "Of course I don't believe in such things, but it's almost as if some supernatural force was punishing these men and women for unexplained crimes," said Colonel Yuwono Malioboro of the Yogyakarta Police.

The victims included:

- Yogyakarta's deputy mayor, Hari Wironegoro, died of a concussion when he slipped on a discarded Starbucks cup while walking from his limousine to the office. Wironegoro was recently charged with fraud when he pocketed the government budget that had been allocated to provide garbage service for slum dwellers.

- An unidentified bearded man, who was a regular visitor to the Parangtritis beach south of Yogyakarta, died after being bitten by his rabid dog. The man, dressed in a dirty singlet and shorts, had been charged three times with stealing from holiday makers and allowing his dog Konyol to defecate on the beach.

- Eight people (an Indonesian driver, an Indonesian guide, and six tourists from the Netherlands, Denmark, and Malaysia) were killed in a fiery explosion when their off-road open-top four-wheel-drive vehicle drove into a chasm while "adventure cruising" on Mount Merapi. Colleagues of the deceased driver recalled that he had a habit of drinking Red Bull and rum, driving recklessly and playing loud rap music for his guests, usually Jay-Z or Kanye West. Photos of the group that were posted on Instagram by one of the dead tourists moments before the crash showed that the two foreign women in the doomed vehicle were dressed "as sluts working in a brothel," according to the tabloid *Yogyakarta Daily Planet*, because they wore bikini tops with "their nipples just about hanging out." Anni Wirabhumi, owner of Mystical Merapi Megatour Adventures, the company that organized the ill-fated excursion, herself died two days later when she used mouthwash that mysteriously contained cyanide.

- When a handsome young man who taught at a public secondary school in Yogyakarta failed to show up for work one morning, his colleagues called his home. His mother told the worried friends that her son had left that morning at the usual time but seemed to be distracted since he hadn't taken his cell phone. A frightened taxi driver said he picked up a man matching the description of the missing teacher around seven a.m. and drove him to the cliffs overlooking the Indian Ocean. The teacher's clothes were later found in a neat pile near the water's edge at Parangkusomo beach. Police are holding the taxi driver for questioning until a better suspect shows up.

***

"The towels are worn. Replace them," the elegantly dressed older woman said.

"Yes ma'am," replied the similarly well-dressed younger woman.

"There is dust and a fingernail clipping under the bed."

"I'll see to it, ma'am."

"And what do you smell in this room?"

"Cigarettes, ma'am?"

"Actually cigar. Very faint. Partagas, I think." She gave a barely noticeable sniff and added, with a touch of Sherlock Holmes in her voice, "A guest lit his cigar inside the room then stepped outside to smoke it. Unacceptable, both his action, and your inability to recognize the problem and notify management."

No reply.

"We'll have to change the curtains, the mattress, and repaint the room."

No reply.

"Too bad that once in a while we get a guest like Mister Johnson."

The maid wasn't sure whether that statement required a "yes" or "no" reply. She said nothing.

"Please pay attention next time and do your job properly."

To an ordinary observer this might seem an exchange between a strict hotel manager and an obedient chambermaid. And it was, on one level. But the younger woman, her long black hair tied in a ponytail and wearing a uniform that wouldn't have been out of place in a film about a seductress working in an exclusive bank, was more than a maid, and the older woman, her hair immaculate in a tight chignon held in place with a diamond and gold hairpin, clothed in a deep green sarong kebaya and starched white jacket and wearing wine-red Manolo Blahnik sandals that matched her lipstick and nail polish, was more than just a demanding hotel owner.

"This guest, this Mister Johnson, did he behave improperly with you?"

The maid hesitated. "Yes, ma'am."

"In what way?"

"He suggested rude activities." The maid used the Indonesian term *kasar*, which means "impolite" or "crude."

"I see. And your reaction?"

"I left quickly and after that only cleaned his room when he wasn't present."

The hotel is called, simply, Southern Ocean Retreat. It has no website. Its phone is unlisted. Its clients include the wealthiest, most powerful, but not necessarily the most visible people in the world. You would know them by their positions, but perhaps not by their names. It is expensive, but money alone does not ensure that a potential guest will get a room.

I know all this because a friend of mine, a professor who is head of the philosophy department at an Ivy League university (he requested I not use his name) was spending a week at the Retreat and invited me to lunch.

The Retreat, not visible from either the main road or

the settlement below, is located on a promontory some hundred meters above the sleepy village of Parangkusomo, some thirty kilometers south of the Javanese royal city of Yogyakarta. Parangkusomo is famed for its wide swathe of black sand beach leading to the eastern Indian Ocean. Heading south from the beach, the next landfall is thousands of kilometers away in Antarctica. It is a dangerous sea in which to swim, and there are many reports of holiday makers who are swept to their deaths by the strong riptides. Particularly vulnerable, according to local beliefs, are men wearing green.

The dining room is an open-air *pendopo*-style area overlooking the stormy sea. The food, prepared by a young Italian chef who would undoubtedly have a Michelin star if his restaurant were open to the public, is strictly vegetarian. I don't have the food vocabulary to adequately describe what we ate; I felt that there were angels helping out in the kitchen. Each timbale, each salad, each quiche, each plate of pasta, each risotto, gave off a subtle essence of the sea, not in flavor as much as in the subtle energy-giving negative ions produced when waves crash on the beach. Our servers were good-looking young men and women, each of whom wore a starched white uniform with a band of green batik on the collar. If you looked carefully you could see that the batik pattern included a figure of a shapely woman's body, which was actually an intriguing combination of the letters that formed the Retreat's name: *SOR*.

I had heard the rumors of course, indeed everyone who has spent time in Central Java has heard tales of what goes on behind the gold and green gates of Southern Ocean Retreat. I had so many questions for my friend, whom I'll call Hal. *What's it like being a guest? It is true that a guest can request a partner for "tantric studies" and that person will read the guest's mind and help him or her achieve otherworldly ecstasy? And who is that chic fifty-something woman on the other side of the dining room speaking with a guest?*

Half an hour to the north, in a comfortable but not luxurious house a kilometer from the *kraton* (palace) of the Sultan of Yogyakarta, the crown princess was having a coffee-and-gossip session (which the practical Indonesian ladies abbreviated to *ko-go* to represent *kopi-gosip*) with her closest friends.

Speaking in a combination of Javanese, Indonesian, English, French, and, when a particularly earthy expression was called for, Dutch, they discussed the eternal themes that occupied the time of such upper-class ladies: grandchildren, business deals, movies, husbands and lovers, the weather ("hot and humid, *again*"), scandals, and lipstick shades. They avoided talking about local politics unless Pembayun herself brought up the subject, at which point each woman had a suggestion.

And suggestions were welcome, because Pembayun was in a pickle.

On the one hand, Pembayun was thrilled. She was going to be the spiritual and cultural leader of some four million people. But with the title came political power as well, since the sultan is automatically designated as governor of the Special Region of Yogyakarta. A woman who previously had shied from the limelight, who had not distinguished herself in academia or business, who had revealed little interest or skill in the often Machiavellian politics of the royal family, was about to become one of the most important of the two hundred sixty million people in Indonesia.

Yet Pembayun was distraught. Few people in Yogyakarta agreed with her appointment as the heir apparent. The move was greeted with anger by the superstitious population of Yogyakarta. "It's just wrong, against our culture," said Soedomo, a local shopkeeper. A Yogyakarta religious leader warned that a female sultan would not be able to officiate at the many Islamic ceremonies required of the sultan. One of the sultan's snubbed brothers grumbled, "The symbol of the sultanate is a rooster, not a hen." A soothsayer said simply, "No good will come of this."

But Pembayun's greatest concern was a conundrum that virtually no one addressed. It was clear-cut, really. Historically, the world over, all sultans, kings, rajahs, emperors, grand dukes, tsars, and emirs enhance their power through a connection with a spiritual entity. Sultan Hamengkubuwono, the tenth in his line, ruled largely because his consort was Kanjeng Ratu Kidul, the mythical Queen of the Southern Ocean. According to legends familiar to every Javanese, Kanjeng Ratu Kidul had helped Senopati, a historic sixteenth-century prince, start the Mataram Dynasty, which includes the royal families in

Yogyakarta and Solo (Surakarta). And Kanjeng Ratu Kidul had pledged to give her spiritual and supernatural support to Senopati's descendants, which included, of course, Hamengkubuwono X and his successor.

The catch is this. As every schoolchild knows, Kanjeng Ratu Kidul is, how shall we say this, *all woman*. According to every tale told about her, she likes men, she appreciates men, she inspires men, she manipulates men.

In a more philosophical analysis one could argue that Kanjeng Ratu Kidul understands that the male/female relationship is not a dichotomy but merely two sides of a continuum. Because she had her origin in Animist and Hindu belief systems, Kanjeng Ratu Kidul represents the balance of forces, the cycles of life, which govern our existence on Earth. Male and female. Day and night. Sun and rain. Hunting and agriculture. War and peace. Exploration and settling-down. Risk-taking and family protection. And to this day, maintaining this type of male/female balance is one of the job descriptions of a Javanese king. He must mediate with nature to ensure that his farmers have sun, but not too much, adequate rain, but not flooding that destroys the crops, biodiversity, but without a plague of locusts. Life is a constant swirl of contradictions, and maintaining the male/female balance in nature is essential if a sultan is to stay in power.

That's the conundrum Pembayun faced. The Sultan of Yogyakarta gets his power from his relationship with the Queen of the Southern Ocean. What would happen if the sultan were actually a strong-willed woman? Would Kanjeng

Ratu Kidul refuse to support Pembayun, thereby signaling the end of a four-hundred-year-old dynasty? Would Pembayun and the Queen of the Southern Ocean fight for power? Or would they get along like two headstrong sisters, sharing mystical duties and responsibilities, perhaps even makeup tips and recipes for *gado-gado*? (Roasted cashews replacing peanuts in the sauce was the hot idea of the moment.)

Kanjeng Ratu Kidul, the respected and feared Queen of the Southern Ocean, is known, at least to my disrespectful friends, as the Mermaid Queen.

In one of many versions of the myth, a beautiful princess from the Padjajaran kingdom was chased out of her palace by an evil stepmother (yes, there are parallels to Cinderella and the Ramayana). In despair, the unfortunate young woman went to Java's raging southern coast to kill herself. While she was performing the necessary pre-suicide rituals, a divine voice enticed her to chill out, enter the ocean, and become reborn as a beautiful aquatic queen.

Meanwhile, Prince Senopati, a very real Javanese ruler, was trying to come to grips with his own emotional challenges. He, too, headed to the southern coast for prayer and contemplation. While sitting on a rock on the dramatic sea cliffs south of Yogyakarta, Senopati was lured into the ocean by the spirit who had become Kanjeng Ratu Kidul, the Queen of the Southern Ocean. During their three-day honeymoon bacchanal in her submerged palace, Kanjeng

Ratu Kidul taught Senopati the secrets of love and the intricacies of good governance.

They exchanged vows and Kanjeng Ratu Kidul promised to be the consort for all of Senopati's descendants – most prominent being the royal lines of the Susuhunan (King) of Solo and the Sultan of Yogyakarta. All great kings benefit from a spiritual connection; in central Java that divine guidance for the rulers is provided by Kanjeng Ratu Kidul. She protects the kings. She protects the sea. She protects Mount Merapi, Indonesia's most sacred volcano that lies just north of the Yogyakarta palace. It is said that a straight, invisible, underwater/underground tunnel connects Kanjeng Ratu Kidul's nautical palace with the sultan's terrestrial palace in Yogyakarta, and in turn with the summit of Mount Merapi. Some suggest this passage is the umbilical cord of the world. It is accessible only to the Mermaid Queen and the sultan.

Like other Asian mythological icons – like Ganesha, like the White Elephant, like Kuan Yin – Kanjeng Ratu Kidul is likely a compilation of cultural greatest hits. Historians (who enjoy scrambling for minutiae and esoteric clues in old manuscripts, crumbling temples, and the hidden corners of their own imaginations) have theorized that Kanjeng Ratu Kidul might be related to the Tantric goddess Tara, to an animistic nature spirit, or to a universal Earth Mother. Maybe all of the above.

The Javanese are a nation of cultural hoarders, hanging

on to dusty ideas and legends that just might, you never know, come in handy someday. Roy E. Jordaan studied the architecture, inscriptions, and legends of Candi Kalasan, an eighth-century temple that is a short distance from Yogyakarta, and came up with the not implausible idea that Kanjeng Ratu Kidul evolved from an animistic spirit that evolved into the Hindu mother goddess Uma (or Parvati, or Durga, take your pick), who in turn morphed into the Green Tara of Tantric Buddhism. Like Green Tara, like Uma/Parvati/Durga, Kanjeng Ratu Kidul has a fearsome side and a benevolent side. (Some wags might suggest this indicates she is the ultimate female goddess, unable to make up her mind). And, like Green Tara, she changes form between an old hag and a beautiful maiden based on the moon's cycle. All the members of this cosmological sorority have a relationship with the sea and with sacred Naga serpents, as well as a reputation as protector of navigators, and all share a fondness for the color green.

But these analyses are rarely clear-cut. We could be making this too complicated.

Kanjeng Ratu Kidul might be something simpler, a nature spirit given human form — in *The Religion of Java* Clifford Geertz says Ratu Kidul is "perhaps Java's most powerful single *lelembut*," referring to her origin as an ethereal spirit. Or Kanjeng Ratu Kidul might be a marine counterpart, separated at birth perhaps, of her twin Dewi Sri, the Javanese rice goddess who is unremittingly terrestrial.

She could be none of these things. Or all of them. The point is that Javanese accumulate beliefs like a chef cooks a curry. A bit of animistic chilli? Of course, throw it in. Some Hindu cardamom, nicely grilled and pounded? Can't hurt. Some Buddhist turmeric, golden and subtle? Absolutely. Some Islamic prayers and Christian guilt? Sure, the more the yummier.

———•••———

"That lady you call the 'chic woman' is Madam Lara," my friend the professor said. "She's the owner, and she manages things."

"Can we meet her?" I asked.

"She doesn't appreciate people approaching her. She'll sometimes stop by a guest's table to see if everything is okay, but the house rule is we wait for her to make the first contact."

It wasn't until we were finishing our dessert that Madam Lara came to our table. When I rose to shake her hand, her grip was firm and she looked me directly in the eyes. I was struck by her hair, luminous black with a narrow streak of blue-gray, pulled tight in a chignon and held in place with a single gold chopstick. We made some small talk about I've forgotten what. And then – I don't know why – I said, "I appreciate the effort you've made to make the resort sustainable." Some platitude like that. And Madam Lara looked at me and instead of thanking me said, "Why would I do anything *other* than respect nature?" She turned to my friend and said, "I hope you will invite your guest to lunch again tomorrow."

Which he did. We didn't see Madam Lara during the

second meal, but as we sipped our espressos, one of the handsome waiters, who resembled a lifeguard in a Javanese version of *Baywatch*, came to our table and said, "Madam Lara invites you to tea. Follow me please."

Her office overlooked the Southern Ocean, which on this day was gray and ominous, with storm clouds quickly moving in. The room was filled with books. Some were antique hand-bound books with spine labels handwritten in *Java Kuno* — the old Javanese language that is a cousin of Sanskrit, but most of the volumes were in English, Dutch, and Italian. Her library included books of modern photography, Asian anthropology, and religion. On her desk sat the latest iMac computer. Next to the computer was a small stone Ganesha. Majapahit period, I thought, perhaps seven hundred years old. A museum piece.

"You write a lot about conservation, Mister Paul. Do you mean what you say?"

"How do you know my name? How do you know what I write about?"

"Ah, don't be afraid. It's not a trick, and it's not a scam. You have to leave your passport when you enter the hotel grounds. Google is the new soothsayer," she said, patting the iMac. "Google knows everything. And of course you have been asking the staff about me. You should know that in Indonesia nothing is secret."

She poured tea from a Javanese earthenware teapot. The beverage was deserving of the small, handleless cups, which were translucent and of the finest Chinese porcelain. I noted a Ming Dynasty imprint on the bottom. I tasted green tea but with notes of honey, lavender, and a slightly bitter, somewhat lemony aftertaste. Soon after finishing the first cup, I felt that I was entering a state where I was relaxed but my mind was attuned to the smallest stimulus.

"You are an interesting woman," I said. "And if I might say so, you have an energy that is rare."

"You are familiar with women's energies?"

I liked the way she turned the word into a plural. Was this woman of indeterminate age flirting? Or was I just kidding myself?

"We face so many problems in Indonesia. And many of them are related to greed and ego. Greed and ego. The two major factors in nature destruction."

I explained I had a similar view. She refilled my teacup.

Are you in a hurry? May I bore you with my view of the role of people and nature?"

And Madam Lara gave Hal and me a thoughtful analysis of why people destroy nature in Indonesia. I wish I had taken notes. I wish I could remember it all. If my memory serves, her philosophy is that people have a need/fear relationship with nature. We come from nature, we are part of the warp and weave of life. But we fear *wild* nature ("Snakes! Spiders! Demons!"), and by extension, we are suspicious of the people who live too close to nature. That has led to a feeling of superiority by well-educated urban folk who watch CNN, whose children can sing Walt Disney songs, who have a preferred latte flavor. The wilderness is dangerous, according to the urban dweller, therefore we have a right, even an obligation, to "civilize" wild nature and the people who live in the forests. "It happened in your own United States," she said. "The white East Coast elite felt it was their manifest destiny to 'conquer' the 'Wild West.' They tried to civilize the Red Indians, and if the natives weren't cooperative they wiped them out. The men afflicted by greed and ego decimated the Indians and slaughtered the buffalo. And the same thing is happening all around us in Indonesia."

We continued to drink tea. I looked at her when she spoke, but by peering into her eyes I could see the beach, where a few people wandered in the dunes. They were a kilometer away, but I saw them clearly.

"It used to be simpler in earlier times," Madam Lara said. "People knew they were people and gods knew they were gods."

"So, you don't buy the New Age philosophy that God resides in each of us? That every person is divine?"

"Of course not. Once you democratize a god then she loses her power to influence."

"And this god, or gods ..." I corrected myself. "These goddesses ... are they benign?"

"They are neutral. They have their responsibilities."

"I never considered that gods have job descriptions."

"Of course you have. You've written about it. Of course many of those job descriptions are man-made — Surya controls the sun, Indra controls the rain, Dewi Sri controls the rice harvest."

And then I realized what she was telling me. The characteristics we humans attribute to the gods have actually been dictated to us by the gods themselves.

"People today don't respect nature. You Europeans use the term "Mother Nature" as if nature is all-giving, all-forgiving. But we Javanese, although we don't use these words, see nature as a lover, a concept to get excited about, but not one to trifle with. Like a lover, nature gives but can also destroy if she isn't treated properly. More tea?"

"Lover Nature." I realized as I said it that the idea would worm into my subconscious.

"You mustn't idealize it. Having a lover implies responsibility. For example, down on the beach right now there might be a man discarding a cigarette packet."

"You see that all over Indonesia," I said.

"Not a big thing, perhaps, but it shows he doesn't give a damn about Lover Nature. And he thinks he can act like that without punishment."

As I continued to look at Madam Lara I also saw, as if in a high-definition CCTV video, a tall Indonesian man take a *kretek* clove cigarette from a packet of Gudang Garam and throw the empty pack into the sand dunes. As soon as the packet left his hand, it somehow reversed position and finished up in his grip. There was a flash, the pack incinerated and the man screamed in pain as his hand caught fire. He was far away. I saw it all.

"And far out at sea there could be a fishing boat trawling with gill nets. Their by-catch includes turtlesand dolphins. They catch sharks and cut off the fins and throw the carcasses back into the ocean."

And again, I looked at Madam Lara but simultaneously saw a fishing boat. Moments before it had been a speck on the horizon, now I could see the entire boat. It was about ten meters long, with a diesel engine belching black smoke. The captain had just given the order to drop the nets when there was an explosion on the boat. The fishermen screamed. Some of them grabbed life preservers or life jackets and leapt into the water. I saw sharks circling. The boat slowly capsized. Several men clung desperately to the hull.

And that's all I remember. I don't remember leaving Madam Lara's office. Somehow I found myself in my comfortable hotel room at the Novotel in Yogyakarta. I was lying on my bed, fully dressed, fully awake.

In due course, Sultan Hamengkubuwono X abdicated and Pembayun became the ruler.

Javanese royal titles are richly symbolic and elaborate.

As Pembayun, her title included the term Mangkubumi, which translates from Indonesian as "the one who holds the Earth." Her formal twenty-two-word regal title included a reference to her ancestor Senopati. She was crowned with the injunction "to bring safety, happiness, and prosperity to the world."

Her title as sultana included Arabic-origin honorifics referring to "strength," "authority," and "rulership."

The sultan had made small but critical changes in Pembayun's formal title so that her designation was gender neutral. Nevertheless, problems of terminology arose. It was confusing enough in high Javanese, and it also created a challenge for English writers, since there is no obvious English term for a female sultan. Which hadn't stopped the English-speaking wags of Indonesia from coming up with suggestions. *Sultanette* had some traction early on, then *Mizsultan* had a brief run. The one that finally stuck was Sultana. It is appropriate grammatically but unfortunate metaphorically, since the sultana's being and appearance did not resemble in the least the dark, dried fruit of her honorific title.

The sultana of Yogyakarta recognized that she had a responsibility to uphold the achievements of other memorable Indonesian female rulers.

Queen Shima was queen regnant of the seventh-century Kalingga kingdom on the northern coast of Central Java. She is remembered for introducing a law against thievery to encourage honesty among her subjects. According to legend, a foreign king placed a bag of gold on the main road to test the famed morality of the Kalingga people. Nobody dared to touch a bag that wasn't theirs, until three years later when Shima's son, the crown prince, accidentally nudged the bag with his foot. The queen issued a death sentence to her own son, but was overruled by one of her ministers who appealed to the queen to spare the prince's life. Since it was the prince's foot that touched the bag of gold, the minister argued, it was the foot that must be punished through mutilation.

The powerful Majapahit kingdom (c. thirteenth to fifteenth century) had three female rulers: Gayatri Rajapatni, Tribhuwana Wijayatunggadewi, and Suhita.

In the fifteenth century, Sultana Seri Ratu Nihrasyiah Rawangsa Khadiyu became the sole ruler of the Samudera Pasai Sultanate of northern Sumatra.

And Sumatra's Aceh Sultanate has seen four ruling sultanas, all in the seventeenth century.

Although they weren't rulers, during the Dutch colonial period Kartini of Jepara and Dewi Sartika of Bandung energized the nineteenth-century Indonesian women's emancipation movement and are considered national heroes.

Megawati Sukarnoputri became Indonesia's first female president in 2001. She was the daughter of Sukarno, Indonesia's first, and most charismatic, president.

The sultana moved from her middle-class house into the *kraton* itself.

She redecorated. She installed solar panels and a waste-water treatment system.

She upgraded the quality of her servants, ensuring they were well-trained, educated, discrete, and had smart uniforms to wear.

She invited Brad Pitt to Yogyakarta to open a new

waste-management facility that transforms garbage into electricity. He accepted. Dwayne "The Rock" Johnson has agreed to fund a faculty of advanced computer technology at Yogyakarta's Gajah Mada University. He will attend the opening. Will Smith has agreed to be patron of the Yogyakarta Arts Council, and Justin Trudeau will be the keynote speaker at the opening of Yogyakarta's Sustainable Cities initiative.

She handles her royal duties to the best of her abilities.

I sought out an old friend, whom I'll call Sita, who is a member of the sultana's *ko-go* group. Ibu Sita is of a certain age and belongs to a class of well-bred, well-educated Javanese ladies who seem to have every aspect of life under control. Ibu Sita is elegant, refined, soft-spoken, and perceptive.

Ibu Sita explained that to the initial surprise of her *ko-go* girlfriends, not to mention the populace of Yogyakarta, the sultana, in her civic role as governor of the Special Region of Yogyakarta, invited a string of local and global environmental non-governmental organizations to set up headquarters in the city. The sultana ordered the city council to write a series of tough laws covering littering, watershed destruction, and riverine protection; equally important she has insisted that law enforcement officials actually enforce these laws. She chairs a commission that has created, according to a *New Yorker* article I wrote, "A new global standard for sustainable fisheries." She has ordered the city's Chinese restaurants to stop serving shark's fin soup. She has initiated Southeast Asia's strictest anti-pollution measures for cars and trucks. She has ordered the dismantling of numerous polluting factories (nine at last count) and constructed mini-rainforest public parks, an example of what she calls "Love Jungles."

Her *ko-go* coffee gatherings continue, but with several changes.

Coffee is still offered, a fine Italian blend brewed on a new Gaggia espresso machine. But the *ko-go* ladies generally prefer to drink Pembayun's "special blend" of green tea, the one with faint notes of honey, lavender, and citrus. While the discussions still include celebrity scandals and the price of mangosteens, the women have formed themselves into a combination brain trust and vigilante committee. The sultana has given each woman a "portfolio" on which to focus, and the women excitedly meet with foreign ambassadors and NGO experts to learn about the latest developments in, say, sewage treatment or public transport. She is patron of several NGOs that support women's rights in the home and workplace. And the women in her *ko-go* group have gleefully turned into eco-spies, alerting the sultana about corruption and abuses of power in government offices that are supposed to protect the environment.

The second major change is the presence of a new member. She is around fifty, and like most of the other women wears her hair in an elegant chignon. She is always immaculately dressed, generally wearing a green batik sarong and a white kebaya blouse. She joins in the *ko-go* discussions with a soft energy and has strong opinions about the breakup of Brangelina, the relative "bad boy" merits of

Matthew McConaughey vs James Dean, the accuracy of the Joyoboyo prophecies, and the future of electric cars. She and the sultana exchange knowing glances during the gatherings, and she often stays behind after the other women have left, to continue their discussions in the sultana's private chambers.

Breaking news from Indonesia:

Incident III:

One clear March morning, a Mr. B. Johnson, resident of the United Kingdom, stepped off his private jet at Yogyakarta's Adisutjipto airport. He didn't quite bounce (B. Johnson *never* bounced), but nevertheless had a verve in his step and a reservation at Southern Ocean Retreat in his pocket. He stood on the top step of the Falcon 2000's retractable stairway and lit a Partagás Coronas Gordas Añejados. Life was good. He had just divorced his third wife, was in line for a top UK government position, and had made a killing (thanks to a touch of insider advice) with his shares in Exxon. He did not notice the tiny pool of water on the top step. His leather-soled right foot slipped and Mr. B. Johnson, a stocky man who could have played rugby had he not been frightened by physical contact, tumbled down the stairway, landing squarely on his mop of blonde hair. The resulting concussion was fatal.

Vietnamese Baker Upsets the French

Joie abounds in a boulangerie of
Ho Chi Minh City.

HO CHI MINH CITY
Vietnam

he problem with a proud nation running an international competition for one of its iconic foods is that you may not get the result you want.

That was the situation at the 34th Grand Prix de la Meilleure Baguette, held in Paris last year. The winner: a jovial forty-two-year-old baker named Nguyen Ngoc Chu, from the outskirts of Ho Chi Minh City, Vietnam.

Few people would disagree with the delight of a French baguette straight from the oven – crispy and golden on the outside, pillowy and unctuous on the inside. How many children, when sent to the *boulangerie* to fetch a baguette for the family's *petit déjeuner*, have returned with a baguette missing a great chunk, torn off in small handfuls by a child unable to resist. Such is a small error of judgment most French parents understand all too well. *La tentation de la baguette*, they might say.

But the victory of a provincial baker from Vietnam, who had never stepped foot on French soil until the competition, upset the Gallic notion of baguette *supériorité*.

The winner came not from a *petite boulangerie* in La Rochelle, not from a medium-sized family-owned bakery in Chambéry, not even from La Tortue Rouge, among the grandest of the classical restaurants on the Seine, where pastry chefs have won *médaille d'or* for everything from *macarons au caviar de cerises noires* to towering chocolate confections. The winner for the best baguette in the world was a foreigner, from a country that the French once ruled and then lost in a bloody and nasty debacle. The winner was a man who couldn't quote Moliere or tell you how many Republics France has had since Napoleon.

The winner was Nguyen Ngoc Chu. I went to visit him.

The competition was a blind tasting. The judges had no idea who baked the baguettes they were eating. I recall an international wine competition held in Paris in the 1990s when, in a blind tasting, a panel of international judges (including two French vinophiles) decided that the French *grand crus* in the competition were inferior to upstart wines from the United States, Chile, and Australia. *Quelle honte! Quel scandale.* But I digress.

Speaking in English, with a smattering of French culinary terms, Nguyen explained that the biggest problem he faced was baking in a strange oven. The kitchen of the

George V hotel is modern, functional, gleaming, and equipped with gadgets that surely must be like a dream fantasy for many chefs. But Nguyen is used to cooking in a simple wood-fired oven. The one he has used for years looks something like a pizza oven, and Nguyen knows, through years of experience, how much (and what kind of) wood to put in, how to regulate the temperature, and where to place the essential pan of water in the oven.

Luckily for Nguyen, the George V has a pizza oven, and for the competition Nguyen took charge of it, much like a French government officer might have taken charge of a Vietnamese province half a century ago.

His secret? Nguyen is deliberately vague. With some interview subjects you have to go slowly, gain their trust. I hung around Nguyen's bakery for a few days, eating noodle soup with him at the small restaurant next door, teaching his kids English when they wandered into his bakery after school. I learned (and am telling you with his permission) that he uses a special wheat flour that has been grown and milled in the foothills of the Himalaya in Pakistan. The yeast comes from a Vietnamese factory near Hanoi, the water is from a pure natural spring in Dalat, Vietnam's premier hill station retreat. He uses sugar grown in Vietnam's Delta region and a pinch of salt, which comes from a box marked Sea Salt, made in nearby Thailand.

Nguyen brought his own charcoal to Paris, made from an endemic and aromatic species of acacia found only in Vietnam's Central Highlands.

One point that particularly upset the judges (once they learned who the winner was) is that in France the baguette is enjoyed more or less *au naturel*, enhanced only with a spread of Normandy butter and some homemade *confiture*. Kids these days like to add Nutella or peanut butter, but that's an aberration of youth.

In contrast, Nguyen's baguettes are a delivery mechanism for Vietnamese sandwiches called *bánh mì*. He sells the baguettes *en gros* to a stream of *bánh mì* women who queue at his shop early each morning. They then fill the golden baguettes with fillings that might include homemade liver *pâté*, mayonnaise, sliced chilli, cilantro, cucumber, pickled daikon and carrot, cold cuts, Chinese *char siu* pork, roasted chicken, crunchy pork skin, and whatever else is on hand. The food critic for *Le Monde* sniffed that "using a baguette primarily to ferry delicatessen ingredients is like using a Ferrari to drive the kids to school."

Nguyen's trophy (a basket made of brass containing six terracotta baguettes) sits on a countertop in his *boulangerie*. I asked him about his future.

"I hear there's an international *escargot* competition every year in France," he says. "We have very good snails here in Vietnam. And twelve varieties of wild garlic. And butter made from the milk of Normandy cows that were brought here in the nineteen-forties."

I ask if that's a serious plan, to expand from baking bread to cooking snails.

"Where is Bourgogne?" he asked.

When It Comes to Love Potions, A Little Dab'll Do Ya

Love-witch in the Philippines has a global
following for her concoctions – you'd
recognize the names of her customers.

SIQUIJOR
The Philippines

1960s ad for Brylcreem hair cream promised "A little dab'll do ya."

Love potion entrepreneur Maria Tambong has taken that slogan to heart and now runs a global business called "Love Dab." But she's not selling a scented hair glop (which is still popular with Filipino dandies). She's selling the allure of instant attraction. Her clients: business people, students, job seekers, and especially politicians. Her product: a love potion "guaranteed to make people like you."

Auntie Maria, as she is known, is one of some fifty *mananambal*, or traditional healers, who live on Siquijor, a rural, half-Singapore-sized island in the center of the Philippines. Siquijor is known throughout the nation as a place of magic;

indeed the official tourism slogan is "the mystical island."

Auntie Maria rose to national fame after a local politician, Rodrigo "Tweety" Estrada Junior, a relative unknown in politics, won a landslide victory in his campaign to be elected governor of Siquijor Province. I enjoyed a grilled fish lunch with him some years ago and asked about rumors that his success was due to the fact that he rubbed a bit of Auntie Maria's love potion on his hand before greeting potential voters. "I don't need a love potion," Governor Estrada said laughing. "You know what got me elected? My enlightened policies. And my killer smile. People like my smile."

While Estrada's smile can't be replicated, the love potion he denied using can be yours for about ten dollars for a small vial.

⁃•⁃

Other Filipino politicians, bereft of policies and good looks, have drifted to Siquijor, an hour's ferry from the regional center of Dumaguette, to buy the clear, odorless, tasteless liquid produced in the backyard by Maria and her three daughters.

Some of these politicians went on to win contests in which they hadn't been given much hope. First Amable "Bambi" Concepcion was elected mayor of Cebu City, then Afonso "Joker" Ayala was elected state senator from Bulacan province. And then people started talking about Auntie Maria as a kingmaker, someone with powers that combined spiritual connections with chemical know-how.

Teddy "Little Bear" Sia was given the post of the Philippines's ambassador to the European Union, surprising many observers since he had never been out of the Philippines and initially thought that Brussels was the capital of the nation of Sprout. Then Tammy "BumBum" Lopez was elected mayor of Makati. Even the recently elected president of the nation, George "Dinky" Sia, is said to be one of Auntie Maria's customers.

Soon industrialists joined the queue of clients. Filipino businessmen, known for their willingness to try anything to enhance profit except honest labor, figured that "if this stuff works for corrupt, personality-challenged politicians, then surely it might work for me." And it did.

———•••———

Love potions have been around since romance has been around. And many people believe that the best love potions are concocted by a witch, traditional healer, or wizard. Believe in the Force and the Force shall be with you.

I visited Siquijor to learn how this island became famous for marketing magic potions.

At first glance Siquijor, population eighty-seven thousand, doesn't appear to be a haven of magic arts. It's as laid-back and as verdant as any out-of-the-way Philippines island. Some seventy thousand tourists a year visit; the Filipino visitors coming for a quick equivalent of a one-day Magical Mystery Tour, the foreign tourists for the pleasant beaches and scuba diving.

With a local history teacher named Abner as my guide, I visited half a dozen healers. We quickly learned that there is no fixed route to health in Siquijor. Several healers, like Marcial Sumagang, a slight man with spiky gray hair and wearing a frayed and faded "Happy Kitty" T-shirt, diagnose by checking the patient's pulse. One woman healer diagnoses by placing an egg on the afflicted body part. Other practitioners apply oil or wood chips. Several healers combine herbal treatments with printed *oraciones* (variations on Catholic prayers). And then there was the "bubble-blowing technique."

When we arrived unannounced at Genelou Magsalay Sumalpong's house, she was nursing her five-month-old daughter. She lives in a comfortable, but not luxurious concrete house, and like most healers has enough disposable income to afford a nice TV and sound system. Abner explained that he had a cyst on his neck. Sumalpong, 24, examined the cyst and got out her simple equipment. She uses a technique called *bolo-bolo*, onomatopoeic for "blowing bubbles," which detects and removes evil spirits that are causing illness. The key mechanism, she explained after some prompting, is the ordinary-looking oblong black pebble that she put into a water-filled jar. Her grandmother found the stone "glittering like a crystal egg sitting on a nest," took it home, and put it on the family altar. That night Sumalpong's grandfather had a dream that he would become a *mananambal*, and a family vocation was born. Sumalpong placed the jar against Abner's neck and blew bubbles through a metal straw. The water stayed clear, and she declared that Abner's problem was natural; no devil was involved. Had the water turned murky with dirt, pebbles, and grass, she would have concluded that Abner had been infested by an evil spirit, necessitating an exorcism.

———•••———

Simply put, "good" mysticism, practiced by *mananambal*, aims to protect and heal. Good mysticisms comes in various delivery mechanisms and is the stuff of herbal massage, traditional herbal medical healing, love potions, tourist souvenirs of "dragon's teeth" concoctions, heart-shaped carved wooden amulets, and colorful plastic bracelets to protect against, as one healer claims, "snake bites, voodoo spells, and vampires."

But Siqujior has a dark side.

"Bad" mysticism, practiced by sorcerers, locally called *mamamarang*, dwells in the world of devil-influenced spells. Way back in the isolated hills of Siquijor, people say, there are *mamamarang* who turn themselves into animals, who talk with the dead and concoct powerful poisons that kill on contact.

What distinguishes "good" from "bad"?

Josette Armiola of the Siquijor tourist office, who acknowledges she "half believes" in magic, says, "Herbal medicines are good. Witchcraft isn't."

Armiola has a powerful ally in her "good/bad" differentiation – the Catholic Church.

Monsignor Larry Catubig welcomed me to his office next to the ruins of a two-century-old bell tower. He acknowledged that the Church has no problem with healers, but does not welcome magicians. I suggested to him that Catholicism, like many religions, is based on miracles. "Yes," he agreed. "Miracles build. But magic destroys."

However Pastor Dario Ocay, a Pentecostal pastor of the Blessed Hope Global Outreach church, has a more draconian view of traditional healing and its associated magic. Sitting in an air-cooled room that doubles as the church's kindergarten, Ocay says, "It's all the work of Satan, and all healers are demon-possessed." Ocay's worldview is refreshingly black and white. He is an articulate and friendly man (he used to be an encyclopedia salesman), who admits that his father was a sorcerer. "All diseases are caused by demons," he says.

"What about something like cancer?" I ask.

"Everyone is a sinner," he answers.

But how bad could the "bad" stuff really be?

Evil enough to kill someone, if Telesforo Lumactod is to be believed.

Abner and I easily found Lumactod's house on the secondary road that runs through the commune of Ponong in the hills about half an hour from the coast. We saw no cars, just a few motorized tricycles and motorcycles. Village life went on at its own sleepy tempo – children played, chickens ran around, shopkeepers languidly chased flies from their produce.

Lumactod wore a green golf shirt and blue denim shorts. He is an unimposing Voldemort, with a wispy Van Gogh-style beard and missing a few front teeth. We disturbed him from his afternoon nap, a sensible pastime in the tropics. He was sprawled on a white plastic chair on the front porch of his concrete house, a half-empty bottle of rum close by.

"Yes, I can kill someone," Lumactod said.

Lumactod's modus operandi for mystical mayhem is not as straightforward as, say, Martha Stewart's recipe for apple crumble. His atelier is a secret cave, where he calls up wandering souls by incanting arcane spells, aided by a picture of the intended victim or a lock of the person's hair.

I thought for a moment about some truly evil people whom I would like to see injured. I decide to let Fate, whatever that might be, take responsibility for their future and do not engage Lumactod's services.

I asked whether Lumactod was worried about what will happen to him after he dies.

"I'm already in hell," the fifty-seven-year-old man says. But the rum confuses him and he rambles. "Heaven is only a story. And anyway, God doesn't give me food."

Lumactod also deals in more mundane love potions and concoctions to ensure business success. Could we buy one of his ready-to-use potions? "Come back later," he says, explaining that his wife handles the retail side of the family business. She is a village counselor, and has gone to town on official duties.

———◆◆◆———

Call it what you will. Healing. Magic. Mysticism. Hucksterism. The work of the devil or affordable health care? How did Siquijor become Walmart of things that go bump in the night?

Perhaps the early Spanish explorers had a sense of the distinctive personality of Siquijor when they dubbed the island *Isla del Fuego* or "Island of Fire," because it gave off an eerie nighttime glow. No matter that this strange light came from the great swarms of fireflies that harbored in the numerous *molave* trees on the island – "Fire Island" has a pleasant metaphysical ring to it.

Vergie Bonocan Miquiabas, author of *The Mystical Siquijor*, says one reason for Siquijor's magical positioning is that people are poor and isolated so they turn to alternative medical healing. "And there are plenty of herbal plants in the forests that provide raw materials for the healers," she adds.

Of course isolation, poverty, and biodiversity occur throughout the Philippines, and other parts of the country have strong metaphysical reputations. But somehow Siquijor has jumped to the front of the queue when people think of magic, and a steady stream of visitors, including high-society matrons and high-government officials, seek treatment and protection from Siquijor's practitioners of the gray arts.

Imelda Marcos, the imperious shoe-collecting wife of The Philippines' President Ferdinand Marcos, was among Siquijor's A-list pilgrims.

In a generally accepted urban legend, the first lady had a skin disease that resisted treatment by the best Western-trained dermatologists in Manila. She consulted a Siquijor healer who explained that Marcos's disfiguration was caused by a curse placed on her by angry mermen (brothers of mermaids) injured during the construction of the San Juanico Bridge linking Samar and Leyte islands. This edifice was hailed as a "love bridge," built in honor of the First Lady by her husband, a sort of modern-day Filipino Taj Mahal. At the urging of a Siquijor healer, the first lady made offerings to the aquatic spirits who lived beneath the bridge, and her skin problem cleared up.

Gossip travels faster than venereal disease in the Philippines, and word of Auntie Maria's love potion reached Erica Fitzpatrick, the American ambassador, a diplomat of the old school who took a real interest in the country in which she was posted. Fitzpatrick is a curious woman who enjoyed exploring the country's esoteric corners. She was considered a bit of an expert (for a foreign woman) on the intricacies of cock fighting, the construction of the Ifugao rice terraces, and the techniques used by wood-carving workshops to make newly carved santo statues appear to be centuries-old antiques worth thousands of dollars.

Ambassador Fitzpatrick sent her secretary Linda Miraflores on a quiet mission to see Auntie Maria, but Miraflores returned empty-handed.

Miraflores is an old friend, and over coffee in a Manila café, she told me what happened.

"I found Auntie Maria's house and met her. She was very nice and offered me tea and biscuits. We spoke about babies and the price of rice, the poor quality of the schools, and village development. Finally she said, 'Well, dear, what do you want?' So I told her I was acting on behalf of an important official and could I please buy a few vials of Love Dab.

"Auntie Maria looked at me carefully and said, 'Do you want the real thing?' I wasn't sure what she meant but said 'Of course.' Then Auntie Maria said that I must come back with the American ambassador herself, that she [Auntie Maria] had to see the person in the flesh, or at least have a lock of hair and a photo, in order to make a powerful potion."

I ordered Miraflores another cappuccino and encouraged her to continue.

"Now the really odd thing is that I hadn't told Auntie Maria that I was there on behalf of Ambassador Fitzpatrick. I had never mentioned the United States, or even that I worked in a foreign embassy."

"So, you think she has extrasensory powers?" I asked.

"I don't know what to think. We Filipinos are very superstitious. I put it down to a lucky guess. But then she really scared me."

I kept silent, waiting for her to continue.

"It's pretty embarrassing."

"You can trust me," I said.

Miraflores took a deep breath. "I promised to come back with my boss, and Auntie Maria said, 'when you come back, bring me a snippet of Jack's hair.'"

"Jack?" I asked.

"Yes, that's the scary part. I knew perfectly well who she was talking about, but I played dumb and asked Auntie Maria who was this 'Jack.'"

Miraflores continued. "Auntie Maria said, 'don't play dumb. I'm talking about Jack, your husband. I'll make up a special potion for him, might help you keep him home at night.'"

I had heard of Miraflores's marital problems but of course had only listened to gossip, never joined in.

"I was flabbergasted," Miraflores told me. "How did she know about my situation? And she knew my husband's name!"

⋯

Ambassador Fitzpatrick and Linda Miraflores went to Siquijor several months later, including it in the ambassador's annual visit to the less-visited corners of the archipelago. Shortly thereafter Fitzpatrick's term was up and she returned to the States as a deputy secretary in charge of human rights in the State Department in Washington, DC.

After a few months in Foggy Bottom, Ambassador

Fitzpatrick left the government and went to work for a number of political campaigns. The people she has advised, including a large number of personality-challenged, loud-mouthed men and women, have all been elected to prominent positions – you'd know their names if I mentioned them. The election of ill-mannered, narrow-visioned people is not new, of course, but in the United States, as in the Philippines, there does seem to be an inordinate number of people devoid of social charm and basic intelligence succeeding in politics. Don't know if there's any correlation, but during the 2016 campaign Ambassador Fitzpatrick worked for Donald Trump as a senior advisor for Southeast Asia.

Fitzpatrick now has a successful, rich husband (her first) – a good-looking historian who is president of Yale. And I've heard that she is considering running for the Senate.

⁂

And Linda Miraflores? I ran into her during a recent visit to the Philippines. After the usual polite talk, I took her aside. "I know it's none of my business, but how are things with your husband?"

Miraflores laughed. "Typical Filipino man. He ran away with his sexy travel agent, leaving me and the baby to fend for ourselves."

"That's too bad. So obviously Love Dab didn't work."

"No, the Love Dab didn't work. But you know Siqui-jor has all sorts of *mamamarang*, and people say some of them can put bad spells on people."

"Linda, you're a good Catholic girl. You're not suggesting ..."

"Seems poor Jack can't get it up anymore with his young lover. And his hair is falling out. And he has terrible acne that he can't seem to get rid of. Constant loud flatulence. And he's got really bad dragon breath that even super-strength Listerine can't eliminate. Poor guy."

Borneo Tree Spirits Go to Court

Rainforest numina accuse the Malaysian government of crimes against nature.

KUALA LUMPUR
Malaysia

"Your honor, I call our ethno-witnesses." At a signal from Andrew Ajang Ledong twelve men and women stood, hesitatingly.

The chief justice, a bemused ethnic-Indian Malaysian named Samuel Aithihyamala, stared over his half-glasses at the plaintiff's lawyer, Andrew Ajang Ledong, then at the group of men and women who had just risen. "Just how many witnesses do you have, Mister Ledong?"

"One for each of the large old-growth trees in the Penan homeland," Andrew Ledong answered. "We're not sure of the precise number, but probably in the region of six thousand."

"You're planning to call approximately six thousand witnesses?"

"No, your honor. That might challenge the patience of the court. I'll keep the number down to a dozen."

"The court appreciates your consideration, Mister Ledong."

The witnesses for the plaintiff had Penan names, but they were not recorded by the court stenographer, a bored civil servant who was tired because she hadn't been sleeping well — she was worried that her husband was cheating with their widow neighbor. The stenographer described the defendants as "Penan witness A, male," "Penan witness B, female," and so on. I did get their names, though: Katong, Ruth. Paya. Melang. Tingang. John. Nari. Gisa. Aiau. Along. Jemal. And Sega. They were shamans, or *dayong*, who could heal and communicate with the spirits. And they represented the Penans' last hope to save their forest.

———◆———

It was the toughest case of Andrew Ajang Ledong's career.

Ledong is a member of the Kayan tribe, one of several indigenous ethnic groups that live in Sarawak, a Malaysian state on the island of Borneo. I was friends with his father, Avalon, a chief's son who years earlier had hosted me in his longhouse on the upper reaches of the Rajang River. Avalon was a keen secondary school student and I was an idealistic Peace Corps volunteer just out of university. Avalon went on to have only one child, Andrew, and made sure the boy got a solid secondary school education at St. Thomas's in Kuching, the Sarawak capital. By virtue of his brains, friendliness, and financial help from a large environmental non-governmental organization, Andrew went to Washington, DC, where he earned an undergraduate degree in political science and a law degree at George Washington University. He was Sarawak's first, and is still the state's leading, human rights lawyer. For decades he has argued on behalf of indigenous Sarawakians who have had their lands confiscated by timber operators. He championed people whose traditional forests had been stolen by conglomerates wanting to plant oil palm and raged in defense of people whose Native Customary Rights had been ignored.

•••

In Ledong's case, "The rainforest of the Tutoh/Apoh/Baram rivers ecosystem versus the Government of Malaysia, the Government of Sarawak, the Chief Minister of Sarawak, Asia Pulp and Paper, Double Bintang Oil Palm Plantations Limited, and Numerous Local Officials," his plaintiffs were the trees themselves, or, to be more precise, the spirits, or *penakoh*, that live in the trees. According to the Penans, who were told so by their shamans, each large tree is inhabited by a specific spirit, described as a numen (plural: numina) by anthropologists. Each numen has a right to exist. It was the numina that occupied the trees that would speak through Katong, Ruth, Paya, Melang, Tingang, and the seven others.

Ledong said that the trees should be granted juristic personhood by the court, just as corporations, governments, and ships at sea are also considered juristic persons, with inherent rights and responsibilities.

Such philosophical concepts are fine, but a legal case requires a specific plaintiff to claim that a specific crime has been committed by a specific defendant.

The crime, in this case, was considered a violation of the innate rights of nature, akin to a basic violation of human rights.

And the specific request? That the entire river catchment area of the Tutoh, Apoh, and upper Baram rivers be preserved for eternity and that application be made to UNESCO to designate the area a biosphere reserve in which the Penans and other resident indigenous groups would have freedom to live in the forest where they could cohabitate peacefully with the forest spirits found therein.

The Penan *dayong* didn't testify immediately.

First, Andrew Ledong presented the conservation problem. He called on scientists, conservationists, and biologists who presented attractive charts and sobering films showing the extent of forest destruction that preceded the seemingly unceasing cultivation of oil palm.

Several of the scientists gave testimony heavy on numbers and statistics — the extent of river pollution and estimates of biodiversity loss. One researcher even tried a "numbers overload," a conservationist's tactic to overwhelm a listener with profuse and complicated statistics. He came up with a dozen different ways to present a single statement.

Since I began my testimony, rainforest half the size of Andorra has been destroyed.

Some of the conservationists chose the emotional (some might say sanctimonious) approach.

One of the world's last remaining rainforests is being destroyed! A rainforest one hundred million years old is being destroyed! A crime against both humanity and nature!

Such testimony went on for a day, often interrupted by angry interjections by the defense lawyers. *That study has not been peer-reviewed! Conjecture! Emotional blackmail!*

The witnesses shamelessly played on the heartstrings of the judges using poignant appeals that conservation groups find work so well with individual donors. Most touching were photos of orangutans that had been hacked to death by oil palm farmers.

Objection, your honor! There are no orangutans in the upper Baram.

"Poetic license," Ledong replied.

"Sustained," said a weary Judge Aithihyamala. "Stick with photos of dead animals from the region in question, Mister Ledong."

Then, Andrew Ledong sought to establish that the Penans lived in harmony with the forest, how their livelihood depended on the forest, and how they only took what they needed.

Ledong put three Penans on the stand. They weren't the *dayong* who would later commune with spirits, but ordinary folks, who Ledong hoped would explain what their daily life was like.

It was the "noble savage" argument of countless conservation presentations.

Unfortunately the Penans were not the best witnesses. At the best of times they had difficulty in explaining their customs, termed *molong*, which characterized their relationship with the forest. Ledong asked them simple questions to elucidate how the forest provided them with food, medicine, shelter, and spiritual sustenance. In spite of Ledong's coaching, it didn't go well. The Penans answered in monosyllables. They were intimidated by the formal courtroom setting and exhausted by the strange food, smells, and noises of the city.

Ledong asked for a break.

He had anticipated that the Penans would need support, so he called on five expert witnesses. These men and women were prominent Singaporean, Indonesian, Japanese, British, and German ethnographers and anthropologists. They had written books about how the Penans lived. They had spent years with the Penans documenting their customs, myths, and cosmology.

This part of the trial got off to a hesitant start with the testimony of Herr Doctor Doctor Professor Helmut Friedrich von Munchausen.

When asked by what criteria the German professor with two PhDs considered himself an "expert witness," the scholar reviewed the dynamics of his academic specialty: *Contra disciplinary solipsism. Ontology as an example of a "toss and turn" dynamic that succeeds interpretive, postmodern, cultural materialist, componential analytic, structural-functional, historical particularist, and unilinear evolutionary turns.*

"It's an easy question," Judge Aithihyamala said. "Where did you study? Did you live with the Penans? Did you write books? Do you teach?"

Judge Aithihyamala, along with his four colleagues who were sharing his burden of judging the case, was eager for lunch. He told the expert to get on with it. Heedless of his scolding, the European offered views on the varying importance of describing the Penan situation: *Animistic, totemistic, analogistic, and naturistic modes of relating to the environment.*

And through it all the defense lawyers smirked. Multi-syllabic jargon flew like debris during a tornado.

Charging like a determined rhino, Herr Doctor Doctor Professor Helmut Friedrich von Munchausen continued: *The Penan situation is affected by the biogenetic structuralism that accounts for the structure of experience. You might know it as the phenomenological "reduction" in the Husserlian sense.*

One of the defense lawyers leapt to his feet.

Objection. The witness is addressing the court as if we are children.

"I will determine the intelligence level of the court," Judge Aithihyamala replied. Then he addressed the witness. "And your point is?"

I will make it simple. There is a liminal warp that mediates two cognized steps of experience — if you would like a simple analogy, consider it a doorway through which various forms of consciousness move from one room to another. Metaphorically speaking, of course.

Of course, a defense lawyer said under her breath.

There are, as you are aware, four agents of warps, often to the point of evanescence. For example, the warp between the waking phase and the dream phase…

⸺◆⸺

To Ledong's relief, after a lunch break (spaghetti Bolognese for Judge Aithihyamala, Hainanese chicken rice for the Penans), the four experts who followed were a bit easier to understand than the German professor.

Ledong asked the British academic expert to describe the Penans' perceptions of nature, and their perceived place in the natural order of things. *Life flow, life force. Acculturation. The inversion of the material world with that of the spirit world.* "Can you summarize in simple English?" asked an exasperated and tired Judge Aithihyamala. The anthropologist did her best.

The Penans have a complex and interdependent relationship with the natural world. They are not "conquerors" of nature, but part of the whole. They follow numerous explicit behaviors so as not to antagonize the spirits of the forests, including specific tree spirits.

"Thank you," a relieved Judge Aithihyamala said. "Wish you had said that earlier, could have saved us quite a bit of energy."

Ledong saw the judges were getting tired, and he hoped his other expert witnesses were competent communicators

According to the Indonesian expert witness: *The Penans*

use their resources sustainably — they call that behavior minut. The spirits insist that people are gentle when dealing with nature, otherwise bad things will happen to wrong-doers.

Not for the first time, one of the defense lawyers jumped up and shouted, just as he had learned to do by watching American courtroom dramas on TV. *Objection your honor! Hearsay! Unreliable witness!* Samuel Aithihyamala generally overruled such objections.

———•••———

The trial continued; the experts testified another full day.

The Japanese ethnographer, a strong-willed but soft-spoken Japanese lady, offered dozens of examples of the competence and yes, the humanity, of the Penans.

Trees bloom in response to the peacock's song. Dozens of wild plants used for everything from curing hangovers to treating snake bite and upset stomach. The Penans predict the time by the sound of the cicadas. They carve precision blowpipes from tropical hardwoods, and make a poison for their hunting darts from the sap of a forest vine. Deceased ancestors are buried in the forest so their spirits could take root as saplings.

Western idealization! The defense attorneys roared; they were, after all, paid high fees for defending the leaders of the nation. *Paternalistic arrogance! Fear mongering! Primitive folk superstitions!*

Most tantalizing was the comment by a Singaporean anthropologist: *During important festivals shamans enter a "dream wandering" trance in which they speak a language only the gods can understand.*

The audience listening to this testimony had no alternative but to feel that the modest Penans were Masters of the Rainforest.

The most touching testimony came when John, one of the Penan elders, who had the triple distinction of having received a secondary school education and who was both a Penan shaman as well as a lay Christian preacher, took fifteen minutes to explain how the forest featured in the Penan origin myth.

The first man and woman, created from trees themselves, learned about sex by watching a branch from a tree entering a hole in a second tree during a storm.

Then came the time for Katong, Ruth. Paya. Melang. Tingang and the other Penan men and women to appear before the court. They were simple people. Ledong had wanted them to wear traditional dress, but the plaintiffs felt that they would be mocked in sophisticated Kuala Lumpur if the men wore loincloths and the women went bare-breasted. So they were dressed in ill-fitting western clothes – dark trousers and inexpensive batik shirts for the men; dark skirts and equally bright batik shirts for the women. Their appearance was like rustics wearing their children's school uniforms. They wore distinctive woven rattan caps decorated with large black and white rhinoceros hornbill feathers (an endangered species, but Ledong didn't think anyone would notice). They couldn't eliminate their tattoos, of course, and the men didn't alter their hairstyles, which featured a bowl cut in front and a narrow ponytail in back.

Ledong's case depended on the testimony of Katong, Ruth, Paya, Melang, Tingang and the others. Would the nature spirits cooperate?

The numina in this case were other-than-human entities that lived in large rainforest trees. These spirits were at the heart of Ledong's case. He needed to prove three things — that the spirits existed, that they had a basic right to exist, and that they would cease to exist if the forest was destroyed.

Over the years Andrew Ajang Ledong fought the good fight on behalf of native peoples and their ancestral homes. His first major case took place in 2001, when Chief Justice Lucas Chin of the Malaysian state of Sarawak decided on behalf of the Iban community of Rumah Nor in a land rights case. Chin realized that his decision would be both criticized and much cited, and he made the effort to explain the history proving that the Ibans had owner-ship of the land. Chin started by analyzing historical tribal ownership patterns, then chronologically dissected the legal situation of indigenous land ownership under the Sultanate of Brunei, the rule of the three White Rajahs of Sarawak, the British colonial period, and finally under the Federation of Malaysia.

One of the defense's arguments was that the Rumah

Nor longhouse was virtually uninhabited. When I visited Rumah Nor, shortly after Justice Chin's landmark decision, only a few old folks were in residence; the remainder of the people who gave Rumah Nor as their permanent address actually lived in the nearby city of Bintulu, where they were able to more easily find work in Bintulu's huge liquefied natural gas complex.

There were other legal hurdles that Chin had to address. One was that Rumah Nor's property boundaries were neither clearly defined nor mapped. Chin addressed this by accepting the plaintiff's claim that oral tradition, coupled with natural markers (a stream, an old tree, a waterfall) could serve as legal proof of ownership.

Another problem was the defense's interpretation of Malaysian law that stated that a community could only claim ownership of land if the land was used for farming. The Ibans of Rumah Nor, like the tribal communities in the rest of the state, generally practiced "static" farming only near the dwellings — fruit, vegetables, rubber. But much larger areas further afield were devoted to shifting cultivation to produce "dry rice" in which the growing area was moved every year, leaving large blocks of land fallow in order to allow secondary vegetation to grow and thereby restore fertility of the soil. According to the defendants, such land was not "used," and hence not "owned."

Chin's decision gave a boost to the now commonly used term Native Customary Rights, or NCR. His decision in favor of the Ibans of Rumah Nor was overturned on appeal. The forces of what Ledong termed "dark greed and unstoppable ego" were too powerful to overcome the arguments of the simple folk of Rumah Nor longhouse.

But no matter how you looked at it, all previous legal cases were based on a Western model of jurisprudence. Spurred on by the cultural and religious beliefs proposed by the three stern, paternalistic desert religions, Western jurisprudence basically takes the view that man has dominion over nature, man has both a responsibility to protect nature but also a right to "make nature productive," and that land ownership has to be proven by Western guidelines.

Andrew Ledong was taking a different view. He was promoting a revolutionary way of looking at our relationship with the natural world. He was challenging the pervasive status of Western jurisprudence with a threatening new legal concept based on ancient truths – ethno-jurisprudence.

In a way, this was a last-ditch effort by Ledong. Nothing had worked previously. Blockades. Negotiations. International pressure. Civil disobedience. Not even the Robin Hood antics of Bruno Manser, the daring Swiss who lived with the Penans for years and had helped them earn international awareness for their cause, had helped. The forces of "development" were just too strong for the beleaguered Penans and their tree-spirit-brothers.

Over a weekend break during the trial, I invited Andrew Ledong to lunch so he could explain his audacious legal approach.

It was not uncommon for indigenous groups world-wide to argue that they had ownership of natural areas that dated back centuries, he explained. Indigenous groups also argued, often successfully, that some natural sites were holy; they became known in conservation jargon as Sacred Natural Sites. The indigenous groups made the case that a particular forest, lake, mountain, meadow, river, or grove had special cultural and religious importance, and therefore should be saved not only for conservation reasons (and there are many such reasons) but also because they are, as Ledong said, "important and, well, sacred."

But that wasn't the tactic Ledong was using in this case.

During the trial Ledong introduced a new legal argument based not on standard Western jurisprudence but on the opposite concept of ethno-jurisprudence. It would not be humans who were fighting on behalf of nature, but rather nature fighting for itself. If you accept that spirits occupy a place or natural feature, you are de facto granting that their abode has an innate right to exist.

Put another way, Ledong's argument was that nature, in various forms, is a "juristic person."

Many (well, to be truthful, most) legal experts scoffed at the ethno-jurisprudence argument giving legality to spirits.

Balderdash! shouted one defense attorney who had learned his courtroom dialogue by watching BBC period dramas.

But during the trial Ledong calmly cited numerous

examples of case law in which Western-oriented courts upheld his approach.

In their national constitutions, Ecuador and Bolivia have recognized Mother Earth as a "legal person."

River systems are often protected through ethno-jurisprudence decisions.

Indian courts have granted "legal person" rights to the Ganges and Yamuna river systems.

In two cases in Ecuador involving pollution of rivers, the courts have stated that the rights of nature prevail over other constitutional rights.

In 2014 New Zealand became the first nation on Earth to give up formal ownership of a national park when it declared that the area, Te Urewera, has "all the rights, powers, duties, and liabilities of a legal person."

In 2017 New Zealand courts ruled that Mount Taranaki is to be granted the same legal rights as a person.

And, also in 2017, after some one hundred seventy years of litigation, a New Zealand court recognized the status of the numina that inhabit each of the more than two hundred forty rapids on the Whanganui River. That judgment, Ledong pointed out, has particular relevance to the Penans' case. Ledong cited the New Zealand court's decision that acknowledged the spirits of the river provide guidance and insight "in times of joy, despair, or uncertainty."

In 2010 the city of Pittsburgh, Pennsylvania, became the first city in the United States to declare nature a "legal person" during a case to ban fracking within the city limits.

The State of Hawaii heard a case in which a Native

Hawaiian shaman testified that the numina that occupy the Mauna Kea volcano on the Big Island would be furious if a telescope was constructed on its slopes. The court ruled in favor of the Native Hawaiian petitioners and the telescope was not built.)

(Such protection is not limited to natural sites. Even inanimate, man-made objects can be protected, provided they are "proven" to be inhabited by spirits. During the British Raj, colonial judges granted juristic personhood status to some deities and their abodes – idols and temples – as long as the deities were consecrated and enspirited during a religious ceremony.)

Shaman Katong was first up. He gave his name, his occupation ("farmer"), age and place of residence. He was one of the last few hundred semi-nomadic Penans, and the question of where his home was located was tricky. "Upper Baram River" was the best he could do. He confirmed that when he went into a trance he wasn't speaking for himself, but merely relaying the voice of the tree spirit. "I have no idea what the spirit is going to say," Katong said. "And I never remember what happened after I return from the spirit world."

Samuel Aithihyamala was a large contemplative man with thinning hair who was proud of his legal prowess and humanitarian approach to the law. He had expected this kind of testimony, and before the trial began had whispered some suggestions to a friend of Ledong's.

Two medical technicians, wheeling a table of medical instruments, strode to the witness box. They applied sensors to Katong's scalp and chest to measure changes in brain and heart activity. He was also hooked up to a polygraph that measured blood pressure, pulse, respiration, and skin conductivity.

"Please explain these gadgets," Judge Aithihyamala said.

"I wish to medically prove that the witness is entering a trance state and is actually speaking with the tree spirits," Ledong said.

"Objection!" roared the defense counsel. "Cheap mechanical charlatanism."

"Overruled," roared Aithihyamala.

Ledong was slightly optimistic, because Aithihyamala was nearing the end of his career and had displayed courage in his recent decisions, sometimes finding against the government and big business.

"Whenever you're ready Mister Katong," Judge Aithihyamala said.

"What have you got there, Mister Katong?"

Andrew Ledong intervened. "These are the accessories he needs to enter a trance." He pointed to the supplies Katong had just unpacked. Clouded leopard's teeth. A smooth stone with a band of quartz running through it. A sliver of petrified wood. A kingfisher feather. Incense made from the sap of a forest liana. Kindling. And a bright orange Bic lighter.

"Sorry, Mister Katong," Judge Aithihyamala said. "No smoking inside a government building."

"Your honor, these, er, things, are essential to help Katong enter a trance," Ledong said.

"Improvise, Mister Katong. Improvise."

Katong held a clouded leopard tooth in his hands, closed his eyes, mumbled some prayers, breathed deeply, and entered a trance. When he spoke his voice changed into a gravelly, rich baritone. His words came out in the Penan language, a novelty tongue rarely heard in cosmopolitan Kuala Lumpur, that was, mixed with birdsong, whooshing wind noises, and chirping crickets.

He clattered the *dtak-dtak-dtak* sound a woodpecker makes when hammering into a tree trunk.

"I don't like this place," Katong said in a deep voice.

Judge Aithihyamala tried to ask a question but was aggressively waved off by Andrew Ledong, who signaled *just wait a bit.*

"Who are you?" Andrew Ledong asked Katong.

"Tree. Leaves. Air. Roots. Flowers. Insects. Moss." Then a slow *whoosh-whoosh-whoosh*, the rhythmic locomotive-like sound of a hornbill in flight.

"Do you know what this is?" Andrew Ledong held up a small chain saw. He pulled the ignition cord, and the aggressive buzz of the tool shook the courtroom.

"Turn it off."

And Andrew Ledong did so.

The nameless spirit spoke in short bursts, sometimes incoherently, sometimes in what sounded like hornbill cries.

The judge wrote a few questions on a notepad and passed it to Andrew Ledong. They were typical "Western" questions. *Where are you? Are you alive? Do you want to be chopped down?*

And the spirit gave indirect "Asian" answers. "I feel the wind." "Squirrels scratch me." The coughing call of a barking deer. The wheezy growl of a clouded leopard.

And so it went until Katong shuddered and slowly opened his eyes.

Not all the shamans went into a trance. Some of them repeated a liturgy, which they called *ba' tara*, that assisted them to enter a beta state by which they could communicate with spirits. However, many of the shamans remained fully alert and lucid and clearly told the court about prophetic dreams they had experienced, or specific bird omens they had seen, which they interpreted as predicting catastrophes, plagues, and disasters if the forest continued to be destroyed.

Throughout the testimony of Katong and other shamans, the defense counsels, well-dressed men and women with impressive college degrees and a higher hourly rate than Katong and the other shamans earned in a year, shouted their favorite combative phrases. *This is a mockery of the law! Next thing you know the plaintiff will be channeling Bruno Manser!"*

And they had a point. If you boiled it down, they were objecting to the complete reversal of the legal system. If the trees' testimonies were allowed to stand, it would threaten the very principles that formed urban Malaysian civilization.

During the trial I sought out the defendants – men and women who were accused of cutting the forest. They were ethnic Malay and Chinese Malaysians, powerful people who had been raised on the idea that man has an *in loco parentis* right of control over "wild" nature, and, by extension, the right of control over the "savage" people who live in the forests.

They had all drunk the "We're doing what's best for the nation" Kool-Aid. The lectures I received were similar to scoldings I have received by people in power throughout Southeast Asia.

You Westerners built your great civilizations because you cut your own forests.

Don't tell us what to do.

We have to help our poor naked cousins the Penans become civilized and enjoy the benefits we city dwellers enjoy.

Don't tell us what to do.

Palm oil is one of the country's most important foreign exchange earners. We need that money to develop.

You care more about orangutans than people.

Don't tell us what to do.

Our farmers grow oil palm following international sustainability guidelines.

You tell us to protect the "lungs of the Earth" but you Westerners do all the polluting.

The rainforest left alone is unproductive.
Don't tell us what to do.

—•◦•—

Eventually Katong, Ruth, Paya, Melang, Tingang, and the seven other men and women completed their testimonies. Some were loquacious. Others couldn't go into trance at all. Few made coherent statements. All, apparently, were sincere. *We exist. Don't kill us. Bad things will happen.*

—•◦•—

The verdict came the following day.

"I empathize with your arguments, but my personal feelings are irrelevant," Samuel Aithihyamala said. "The law is clear. Spirits have no legal standing in Malaysia. Decision for the defendants."

The defendants and the defense lawyers punched the air, packed their files, and made plans to celebrate that night at a large and garish Chinese seafood restaurant in Kuala Lumpur, where the brandy would flow, the shark's fin soup would be ladled, and the men in the group would smoke large cigars, as they had learned to do from watching *Boston Legal*.

So that should have been that. The Penans, used to generations of disappointment and being ignored by the powers that be, packed up their few belongings in simple but elegant rattan backpacks, and prepared to return home.

Except just then, as people were filing out of the air-conditioned courtroom into the humid heat of a Malaysian afternoon, Ruth went into the deepest trance witnessed during the trial. She stood rock-still, arms outstretched, and roared. To say it was an unearthly roar would be misleading; it was a roar *of* the Earth. To the Penans, it was a sign, surely.

———•••———

I wish I could say that Ruth's lament of the tree's discomfort led to a hurricane that destroyed a timber camp, or a deadly accident for one of the government officials, or a plague of venomous snakes that attacked non-Penan intruders in the forest. I wish I could say that Bruno Manser's ghost appeared, Banquo-like, to shake things up.

As far as I know, none of these things happened. The forest is still being destroyed. Ruth, it is said, still wails, but with less vibrancy than earlier.

The Sordid Side of the "Land of Smiles"

UN Human Rights Commission investigates Thailand for "systematic and ingrained racism" against Caucasians.

PATTAYA
Thailand

"**T**his is an outrage!"

I raise a skeptical eyebrow.

"We are *not* racist. Not at all," declares Jidapa Thitiwattanakan, head of Thailand's Department of Public Perception.

We are in the delegates lounge of the Palais des Nations in Geneva, Switzerland, where an hour earlier Thitiwattanakan had been interrogated by the United Nation's Human Rights Council, the investigating body of the United Nations Commission on Human Rights. The charge: egregious racism against white foreigners.

How could this happen to a country that bills itself as "The Land of Smiles"?

Thailand has a dark side. The kingdom, which regularly ranks among the top ten in global tourist arrivals, has been investigated by the United Nations Human Rights Council for crimes as varied as forced labor in the fishing industry, mistreatment of seasonal workers, trafficking in women, forcing underage girls and boys into sex work, unsafe working conditions, and denial of basic residency documents and benefits to thousands of refugees from neighboring Myanmar who have lived for decades in refugee camps along the Myanmar-Thailand border. Often, much publicized violent crimes against white foreigners have been blamed on Asian foreigners (Burmese are often handy scapegoats) to draw attention away from more likely Thai aggressors – witness the setup of two young Burmese men for the murder of two British tourists on the Thai island of Koh Tao in 2014.

"Thailand is bipolar toward foreigners. They like foreign money and some aspects of foreign culture but don't particularly like foreigners as people," says Patrick Murphy, founder and lead gadfly of the protest group FARANG (Foreigners Against Racism And Nasty Government) who brought the suit to the UN Human Rights Council.

The official FARANG complaint said that the people of Thailand, supported by government actions (and inactions), have caused "pervasive and ingrained prejudice against Caucasian visitors and residents, resulting in physical, economic, and emotional hardship."

———•••———

Murphy, an articulate and bitter Irishman from County Cork, was busy trying to buttonhole Human Rights Council delegates when I interviewed him in Geneva. He was polite but rushed and couldn't take the time to properly explain why his group has sought legal recourse against Thailand.

I sought him out a month later in his single room on a back street in the Thailand seaside resort of Pattaya.

I consider Pattaya to be one of the vilest resort cities on Earth. It's a haven for overweight, under-brained foreigners in search of cheap beer, dicey drugs, and sexual thrills (besides the usual girls and boys, Pattaya is a world center for transvestite (*katoey* in Thai) hookers. Scammers abound (one favorite ploy is for a Thai vendor to claim that a visitor has damaged a rented jet ski, and then demand excessive compensation by refusing to return the tourist's passport that had been left as collateral). Pattaya is Sodom and Gomorrah on an Asian scale. An ugly, nasty resort on a polluted bay. Lots of foreigners love the place.

Murphy is a tall, slightly pudgy seventy-four-year-old former police detective from Dublin. After an acrimonious divorce from his Irish wife, he moved to Thailand in 2006 seeking "a less stressful life in a country with nice people, good food, and respect for older visitors."

"What people don't realize," Murphy added, "is that behind the tourist-enticing blah-blah-blah, the Thais have a dirty secret."

I raised an eyebrow.

"They're racist."

"That's a pretty strong statement."

Murphy outlined his argument. The Thais use the term *farang* to describe all white foreigners, regardless of their country of origin (with different, and often even less flattering names for Chinese, Japanese, Arabs, and Africans). According to Murphy, *farang* means "foreigner," which by definition is exclusionary. "When I walk down the street, mothers with little children will point at me and say *farang*," Murphy said. "Every day, countless times, people mumble *farang* to me. If I stumble on the broken pavement, the Thais say, 'The *farang* can't even walk down the street.' If I'm eating at a food stall, people will say, 'the *farang* can't eat spicy.' Or "The *farang can* eat spicy.' Either situation is worthy of racial comment. When I hear things like that I tell them it's not polite, but they shrug and look at me like I'm from Mars. Policemen fine me for dropping a cigarette butt on the ground but ignore the same action by Thais. Taxi drivers try to cheat me and say in Thai 'stupid *farang*.' I get overcharged in shops. They don't know I speak Thai and I scold them, and they curse at me."

Murphy went into the tiny kitchen and came back with a couple of cold Singha beers and some green papaya salad, sticky rice, and roast chicken he had picked up earlier from a street vendor. "Can you imagine if a foreign-looking person walked down the street in any European city?" he asked. "Would mothers point him out to their children and say 'look at the Asian!' It wouldn't happen. We Westerners have basic good manners, the Thais don't. I've asked dozens of cosmopolitan, educated Thais whether they have ever had this kind of racism happen to them when they travel. They say, 'No, we've either been treated politely or ignored. We've never been singled out as being different.'"

Murphy continued, obviously rolling out arguments that he's made numerous times before. "Do you remember when a British family — elderly parents and an adult son — were beaten up in full view by Thai thugs on the main street of Hua Hin? Nobody intervened to help them."

The term *farang* has uncertain origin. One explanation is that it derives from the Thai pronunciation of *français*, as the French played an important role in Thailand's history. Other attributions suggest it might come from the Hindi word *firangi*, a derogatory term for Europeans that was coined during British colonial rule in India, or from the Persian word *farang* or *farangī*, meaning "Frank, European," which in turn comes from the Old French word *franc*, a Germanic tribe during the early Middle Ages that gave modern-day France its name. It might come from the Arabic word *afranj*, which means white/European people — this term has a distinctly negative connotation because the Arabs used it to describe European crusaders. And the Chinese used the term *folangji* to refer to the heavily armed (and heavy-handed) Portuguese sailors when they first arrived in China.

Murphy was actually referring to a universal phenomenon – every language group, nation, religion, ideology, and culture has its own jokes and slurs based on gender/ethnicity/social class/fashion sense/faith. Everybody knows what these terms are, and most people avoid using them in proper company. In Thailand, as in virtually every society, the term "foreigner" equates with "an other," which equates with "strange/stranger," which equates with (usually negatively) "someone different to the standard." Negative descriptive terms (and most of them are negative) are the fuel of xenophobia, mistrust, and sometimes violence and human rights abuses.

What is surprising, as Murphy pointed out, is that Thailand is considered by the outside world as being unrelentingly "nice." The common belief is that people smile. People are polite. The food is good and cheap. It's a tropical country with plenty of air-conditioning, and the shops are filled with anything you might want to buy. A delightful place to visit.

The "us" vs. "them" dichotomy in Thailand is pervasive partly because of strong nationalism. It is a country where folks brag that they have never been colonized, and where the reaction to any kind of external criticism is usually "no foreigner can understand 'Thai-ness'." This attitude came to the fore when Australian chef David Thompson, owner of Michelin-starred Thai restaurant Nahm in London, decided to open a branch in Bangkok, vowing to serve authentic and historically accurate Thai food. Some Thai socialites were aghast, others gave him grudging credit. From my point of view (but what do I know, I'm not Thai), Thompson has done Thai cuisine a huge favor. He speaks and reads classical Thai, and he has a library of hundreds of books containing recipes and menus from centuries past. He is a historian as well as a talented chef. He discovers historical tastes that other modern Thai chefs have not investigated. Good for him.

Murphy was on a roll. "The Thais will jump in front of you in a queue like you're not there, and they are never scolded by the shopkeeper, who serves them first. They refuse to standardize the Romanization of the language, making it extremely difficult for a foreigner to learn to read and write Thai. I could go on and on," he said.

Murphy took a gulp of his beer and continued. "Even my Thai wife called me *farang*. She mocked me when I wanted to eat steak and kidney pie, or oysters, or spaghetti carbonara, calling them *farang* foods. If I was watching the BBC, she'd complain and say, 'I don't want to watch *farang* TV.' She said she was just joking, but there was an edge to her voice."

"That's the basis of your complaint to the Human Rights Commission?" I ask.

"Not at all, those are the outward symptoms. Our complaint is based on the fact that foreigners can't own property in Thailand and that every foreign man [I note that Murphy carefully refuses to use the term *farang* to refer to himself and his cohorts] married to a Thai woman has zero rights to the property that he has paid for. I have dozens of legal affidavit statements of men who have lost everything. These are men who have been kicked out of the homes they bought with their life savings by greedy Thai women who realized that the law would protect the Thai and screw the European. These men are left penniless, heartbroken, and often turn to drugs. Some kill themselves. It's tragic. Shakespeare could have written a play about how the so-called legal system in Thailand abuses the rights of foreigners."

Murphy said he doesn't want this complaint to be about him, but he has had a tough time of it in Thailand. He explained that after he ended his thirty-year marriage in Ireland, he came to Thailand and enjoyed the lifestyle and the attention of a bar girl nicknamed Noi. "She was a good girl, or so I thought," he said. "Poor family. Big family. She didn't like what she was doing, but she had to support her family — her father disappeared right after knocking up her mother."

Murphy pointed out that the bars of Thailand are filled with foreign men paired with local women with similar hard-luck stories. I made the appropriate "tell me more" noises and Murphy continued.

"We bought a nice little house near the river in Buri-ram," he said. "Of course I paid for it and she owned it. Biggest mistake of my life."

They were happy for a couple of years, Murphy said, but "then Noi turned on me. I'm not sure why. Maybe she got tired of me, or there was someone else. Who knows?" Murphy is tearing up now. Seems Noi, the love of his life, the woman for whom he left Ireland, dumped him.

"It was messy. One day she returned to the house with a couple of thugs. Her cousins, she said." They beat him up. Threatened to kill him if he made any trouble. Stole his laptop, passport, and bank account book. Gave him one hour to pack his belongings and get out of "Noi's house."

All Murphy has now is an Irish pension. It's enough to meet his survival needs, but not enough to fill the hole in his heart. "I lost my wife who I thought loved me. And my kids in Ireland have disowned me and won't speak to me."

But how can this be? I asked Murphy. Thai women have a reputation for being demure, obedient, sensual, and attentive, putting their man's needs above their own.

"It's bipolar," Murphy explained. "In Theravada Buddhism women are second-rate creatures — men can head straight into Nirvana when they die, provided they've laid the groundwork by making the necessary merits. But a woman's only option is to live a good life and hope to move up the ladder and be reborn as a man the next time around."

I didn't understand what this had to do with his personal situation, but I let him continue.

"Thai men are entitled bastards. Most of them drink, some of them beat their wives, all of them cheat. That's why many Thai women like foreign men. We treat them well. And we're generous." He stops to get some cold beers for us. "Maybe too generous. My wife's family looked at me as a walking ATM. You have no idea how many times her grandmother had to have a life-saving operation, or how many cousins needed university tuition, or how many water buffalo have died and need to be replaced before the next rice planting season."

Murphy has a point. A 2016 study showed that about half of married Thai men commit violence against their spouses. More than seventy percent of Thai men have multiple secret sexual relationships, and a 2012 study (by condom manufacturer Durex) found that Thai men are the most unfaithful lovers in the world, with fifty-four percent of respondents admitting to having affairs.

I later sought out Jidapa Thitiwattanakan, the Thai government official I had briefly met in Geneva. She was polite, but scoffed at Murphy's complaint. "True, we are a proud people," she said. "We value Thai traditions and culture. We open our hearts to everyone who comes with *jai dee*. Good heart – good intentions, good values, good motivations – that's what counts in the Kingdom."

"Patrick, I don't think you're being fair," I said. "I know dozens of foreigners – both men and women – married to Thais. Most are reasonably happy." I suggested that his situation was an anomaly.

"No, no, it's common," Murphy insisted.

I suspected Murphy wasn't giving me the entire story. Was there a triggering incident, perhaps an indiscretion on his part?

Murphy mumbles and misdirects. "No, I'm a victim," he said. This was an interview, not a court of law and I let it drop. But if Murphy had committed adultery, he's lucky that all he lost was his house since Thai women are notorious for cutting off their husbands' penises in retribution for adultery – the act is called *tdat joo hai bhet khin* (cut the dick to feed the ducks). Some one hundred cases were reported from 1973 to 1980; all the mutilated men were Thai. Most of the knife-wielding women were not prosecuted. And in spite of the much-touted skill of Thai surgeons to reattach severed male organs, most such surgeries are unsuccessful. According to news reports and urban legend, most detached organs are fed to the farm animals or flushed down the toilet, although one visionary woman attached her husband's severed member to a gas balloon so it would fly so far away he would never be reunited with it. And a culinary-oriented wife allegedly put her husband's member into a grinder and cooked the minced meat in soup.

I leave Murphy in his dismal room and head toward my comfortable seafront hotel with a view of the bay, where tourists scream around on jet skis and bored Thai youths ogle scantily clad European sunbathers. I get no further than a few steps from his building when a *tuk-tuk* pulls up next to me. "Hey mister," the driver says. "You want girl? Boy? Ladyboy? Rubies? Hash?" I refuse politely, in English. "Why you say 'no'? All *farangs* want something."

My Thai isn't bad and I scold him in that language saying "*Farang* is a disrespectful term. Why don't you say 'visitor,' or 'guest' or even 'foreign friend,' like they do in more civilized countries."

He looks at me like I'm crazy. Under his breath he says, "Stupid *farang*" and drives off in a burst of purple exhaust.

Rusty Nails Derail Magical Mystery Tour

World's first university for sorcerers
opens in Indonesia and gets hit by
"black magic" shamans.

SOLO
Indonesia

have achieved one of my professional ambitions. I am a professor at an institution of higher learning.

But my tenure might be short-lived. My academic home is under attack by mystical, rusty-nail-wielding shamanistic terrorists.

A bit of background is in order.

I'm associated with the ASEAN Graduate Institute of Sorcery and Healing (AGISH), based in central Java.

"Throughout Southeast Asia there are thousands of sorcerers," says Heru Darmawangsa, provost of AGISH. "But up until now there has been no way to separate the qualified healers from the charlatans, no way to separate the witches who deal in white magic versus those who practice black magic. The consumer is confused."

As the AGISH website explains, each country has its own tradition of sorcerers. They go by many names – *dukun* in Indonesia, *bomoh* in Malaysia, *mananambal* in the Philippines, *moh phii* in Thailand. These men and women play important roles in society.

"They help heal people suffering illnesses – both physical and mental. They give people a sense of protection and confidence. They even encourage people to fall in love. If sorcerers didn't exist, we'd have to invent them," says Sylvie Witoelar, an AGISH professor of Potions and Traditional Treatments.

◆◆◆

As anyone who has read Harry Potter knows, the "white" arts are always complemented by, and often in conflict with, the "dark" arts. The borderline between "good" and "bad" can be fluid and indistinct. Put simply, the "white magic" taught at AGISH was seen as a threat by the practitioners of the "dark" arts. Chaos ensued.

◆◆◆

Like most institutes of higher learning, AGISH faces inter-faculty disputes. Most vitriolic was a turf war several years ago between the Faculty of Potions and Traditional Treatments, the Faculty of Amulets and Charms, and the Faculty of Religious Mysticism. All three groups claimed the right to teach the use of coprolites (*duk dae hin*, or "stone butterfly chrysalis," in Thai), the fossilized corkscrew-shaped dung produced by sharks two hundred million years ago during the late Triassic period, when what is now Thailand's northeastern plateau was under the sea. The Faculty of Potions and Traditional Treatments, arguably the most powerful faculty because its remit includes herbal remedies, argued that, when ground and mixed with other ingredients, coprolites become powerful protective potions, and thus deserve to be taught by their faculty. No way, contended the Faculty of Amulets and Charms, whose outraged teachers pointed out that coprolites are commonly used in their intact form and worn as protective amulets. Then the Faculty of Religious Mysticism joined the fray, noting that coprolites have perceived power because their appearance reflects the conch shell of Vishnu, one of the main Hindu gods. When blown as a trumpet, the conch produces the *Om* vibration that is the sound of the creation of the universe. The conch was later appropriated as one of the eight auspicious Buddhist symbols. "And since the beloved king of Thailand is seen as an avatar of Vishnu, well, you do the math," noted Father Joseph O'Brien, professor emeritus of the Faculty of Religious Mysticism.

At the time I write this, the matter is unresolved and has been sent to the dean for adjudication. The file has been sitting on her desk for a long time, and all three faculties continue to claim fossilized shark dung as part of their domains.

————•••————

But these inter-faculty disputes pale in comparison to the attacks by what AGISH officials have called "the dark forces."

Beginning six months ago, an AGISH lecturer (for privacy concerns I won't give the names of the victimsin these incidents) suffered severe abdominal pains. An X-ray showed her stomach contained four nails. Implanting foreign bodies is a well-known tactic of "black arts shamans." The nails were removed by a surgeon in Yogyakarta, who said he and his team handle about ten such cases a year.

Shortly thereafter, a graduate student in the Faculty of Fame and Fortune had a similar incident — six sewing needles were removed from her lungs.

And then the attacks escalated. One faculty member had violent spasms of coughing up blood mixed with a noxious green slime. One student became impotent, another lost his hearing. A senior administrator's house burned down; she lost most of her possessions.

No one claimed responsibility.

————•••————

The basic AGISH course is a Certificate in Magical Mysteries, which generally requires six months of training, some of which can be done online. This introductory-level course, heavy on history and light on practical applications, offers "insights into the background and practice of good magic throughout Asia." It is "absolutely not based on the marketing model of Trump University," according to Dean of Admissions Sita Panggabean. "Our business model is completely above board, as are our finances. And, unlike Trump University, we have a large scholarship fund for underprivileged young people with potential supernatural talent."

However, people who want to practice as sorcerers (and the term, as defined by AGISH, is non-gender related) must complete a rigorous two-year residential course, which leads to a Diploma of Practicing Sorcery. These courses are run in partnership with internationally recognized institutes of research and higher education, including the Naropa University (for spiritual underpinnings), MIT (for research into altering cell structure through intention, and generating personalized magnetic fields), and the Royal Academy of Dramatic Arts (for performance training). The curriculum is practical; we do not seek to push the frontiers of academic knowledge, but rather train men and women to use the spiritual arts for healing. We've got tutors from the Natural Institute of Radiological Sciences in Chiba, Japan, who teach our students how to direct and enhance the power of their *qi*, Tibetan Buddhist monks who teach deep meditation, and healing experts from the University of Pavia in Italy who use mantras to generate "compassionate intention." And we've even flown in Native American shamans who teach the power of drumming to enter altered states.

Practitioners can then elect to pursue graduate specialties, much like medical doctors. On offer: advanced degrees in teleportation, exorcism, faith healing, communication with souls that have passed on (one of our most popular specialties), and removal of evil spells.

———•••———

Evil spells have always been a problem facing white sorcerers.

Throughout Asia I've found that many (dare I say most?) educated people have stories to tell in which someone had an interaction with a spirit. Sometimes these involve vague hearsay — someone heard it from her cousin who heard it from her hairdresser who swears it happened to her brother's football coach. A man wearing a blessed amulet walks away unharmed from a major car accident. A soldier is shot and the bullet bounces off his amulet-protected chest. A plain, older woman snares a successful, rich, much younger businessman as a husband and quickly bears him triplets (all boys, bien sûr). A woman has a spell put on a sexy singer who has been sleeping with her husband — the singer's hair and teeth fall out and her body odor smells like rancid shrimp paste left too long in the sun.

It's easy to dismiss these as superstitious rumors. But people believe them, which makes them real. And I've seen some of these spells in action. What are they? No idea.

———•••———

The "dark forces" are not the only problem facing AGISH. Indeed many of our problems result from our own hubris. Dean of Admissions Sita Panggabean acknowledges some of the problems AGISH faces. "Traditionally, shamans and healers are taught by oral tradition," she notes, and many of our students have little formal schooling and aren't comfortable receiving information via lectures or by reading. To be honest, the majority of our most talented students are illiterate. And of course many of the people who are potential clients of shamans are also illiterate. The written word isn't terribly important to them; both shamans and clients rely more on emotions, non-verbal actions, reputation, and performance."

I realized this during my early days as tutor in the Faculty of Performance. My worldview of communications relied heavily on PowerPoint and writing catchy slogans. I soon learned the need to develop the often subtle (but sometimes blatant) methods good sorcerers use to generate confidence. We teach our students to train their voices when they go into trances (the Faculty of Trances and Altered States includes voice and acting coaches). What clothes to wear (there is an ongoing debate about whether flamboyant argus pheasant feathers are excessively showy). What kind of supporting material – things like magic stones, animal skins, incense, rattles – they might use. And, critically, how to handle the delicate question of remuneration – what to say when the client says, "How much do I owe you?"

Other problems include a language challenge – AGISH has faculty from several European countries, Japan, Thailand, Cambodia, the Congo, Gabon, the United States, Myanmar, and Indonesia, and we have to have a variety of translators on staff.

Panggabean adds that "At the beginning we accepted students who were only taking our courses so they could claim to be a trained shaman and make a lot of money.

"And we severely underestimated the importance of natural ability in selecting our students," she says. "It's a bit like finding a composer with innate skills like Mozart, or an athlete with a basic ability and determination like, say, Michael Jordan or Reinhold Messner. While everyone has *some* shamanic potential, some people are born naturally gifted. We should have been more diligent in seeking out true, innate channelers, the men and women who are likely to become Hall of Fame shamans. But we've gotten better. To a certain extent we can employ psychological tests and background interviews to find people with metaphysical potential – musicians who have vivid nightmares often have innate shamanic skills, for instance."

———•••———

And attacks came from other camps. Fundamentalist religious groups, of various denominations, attacked our school as heretical, the "work of the devil," and condemned us to their particular versions of hell. But, in a conversation we've often had in the faculty lunchroom, are there really such big differences between what we teach and what religious priests advocate? We're all on the same path, seeking to enlist higher forces for the benefit of humanity.

———•••———

"Our goal is that consumers, when searching for a magician, will choose those people who have graduated from our program," Panggabean says. "Our expectation is that people will look for the AGISH mark of credibility and serious purpose."

------◆◆◆------

The people wielding dark forces are our main problem and continue their mischief. Last week a group of second-year students went amok and attacked a group of graduate students, who had been put under a similar spell. The second-year students shouted incantations and sacred mantras. The graduate students retaliated with sacred flying kerises and ancient Tantric curses. Voodoo dolls were waved about. Garlic was consumed.

I asked AGISH's president, Hiroki Matsuyama, what had happened.

"It was like they had all been taken over by evil spirits," he said, explaining that senior faculty members were immediately called in. "They started a son et lumière *fogging procedure," he said, referring to an emergency technique used to quell disturbances caused by too much negative energy in the environment.*

And did that work?

Matsuyama is an old friend, and he takes his time answering questions, perhaps to make his answers seem more important. "Well, the sacred smoke was so dense it caused a helicopter crash," he said after a long pause. "Luckily the chopper was just taking off so injuries were limited to a few broken bones."

"No, I meant what happened to the spellbound students?"

"Well, the sacred smoke knocked them all unconscious for a few minutes, and when they recovered they couldn't remember what had just happened. It all sort of blew over," he said, laughing at his own joke.

I asked what he thought had taken place.

"You tell me," he answered, quickly this time. "But for me it's clear. The dark forces had somehow broken through our psychic protective screens and entered the students' bodies."

"There's something you're not telling me," I prodded.

"Well, don't spread this around, but when we debriefed the infected students, we gave them X-rays. Know what we found?"

"Nails?"

"Worse. Each of the infected students had a little brass amulet of a crocodile in the stomach. When the doctors removed the metallic objects they wriggled, like a fish out of water."

"So, how vulnerable are the rest of us?" I asked.

"Hard to say. We've reinforced the outer psychic boundary of the university, and we've given all students and staff special protective mantras to recite. And, if anyone wants it, we are offering to insert tiny amulets of Kali into their upper arms."

Kali, I knew, is seen as a Hindu destroyer of evil. Although she is often pictured as wearing a garland of skulls, she is a powerful protective and positive force.

"So, we're on the defensive."

"Officially, yes," my friend said. "We're victims."

"But surely we're going to retaliate?"

Matsuyama smiled. "Of course. It's time to stop singing Kumbaya and hanging out in a smoke lodge. We've been kind and gentle for too long."

The story was getting more and more interesting.

"You might have heard the rumors," Matsuyama told me, after looking around to see if anyone was listening. "We have some double agents — black magic practitioners who are worried about their karma and want to join the white side. Don't be surprised if, in a short while, you start to hear of cases where nasty, unrepentant black magicians are found wandering aimlessly, naked, babbling, oozing puss from their orifices, and singing Disney cartoon songs."

Harriet and the Monk

American pilgrim in search of "ecstatic enlightenment" seeks "sky dancer" status in a Bhutanese cave.

She has been called a "guru groupie." A "sadhu sycophant." A "fakir fucker." A "shaman shtupper." A "rishi romper." A "hermit humper."

None of the taunts, whispered behind her back, *bien sûr*, bothered her. She had a different term to describe herself, in those rare moments when she indulged in self-reflection. Pilgrim. A seeker of truth. Which, as we all know, can come in a variety of guises.

I first met Harriet Rabinowitz in the 1970s at a café in Ubud, at a point in her life when she was still testing the waters of her ability to absorb new forms of enlightenment. We were sitting at adjacent tables and had a pleasant, rather precious chat about the Ubud vibe – "amazing energy," we agreed, but "Ubud's changing fast." Shallow talk about whether the fruit juices were better here or down the street. There was no physical attraction on my part, and I suspect the reverse was also true. Harriet was trying a bit too hard to position herself, with her unkempt hair, granny dress, John Lennon sunglasses, and unshaven armpits. Her heavy Chicago accent put me off. She had a disconcerting way of looking at the ground when I was speaking and then suddenly raising her head and staring at me as if I was saying something of great import that she wanted to absorb completely. Everybody talks to everybody in Ubud, at least they did in the 1970s. I had just spent a few minutes looking at the offerings on the café's bulletin board and asked if she had any suggestions about what yoga classes might be suitable for a keen, but basically lazy soul like myself.

I ran into her a few days later at a different café ("better brownies here," she said). I told her my difficulty in twisting my body into the required postures and my lack of patience with the whole meditation gig. She scolded me and said something like, "The journey isn't smooth for arthritics," and dug out that chestnut about "when the student is ready the teacher will appear."

"And has the right teacher appeared for you?" I asked.

"Still looking."

Like Harriet, I had finished university a few years earlier. I had considered two career paths — psychiatry or journalism. I quickly realized that the professional techniques of the two disciplines are similar — ask a probing question then sit back and listen. Don't fill in the empty spaces. Keep the flow going by saying, "I see," and "How did that make you feel?"

Two brownies and a slice of mango cheesecake later,

Harriet told me about her experiments with acid and grass at the University of Chicago (major in eastern philosophy and a minor in Sanskrit), how she felt "different, even superior" to her classmates and friends, her desire to go on a hero's journey, "like Jack Kerouac," to find her "true path."

It was a time when soulful exploration included sexual adventuring. Harriet told me about her lovers who helped her on her journey. There was her philosophy professor who liked to quote Plato during foreplay, her LSD pusher who dressed up in animal costumes during their trips, the much-bearded poet slash songwriter slash motorcycle mechanic (*Zen and the Art of Motorcycle Maintenance* was very big back then). She learned from each of them.

I kept in touch sporadically with Harriet, and also with her sister Freda, a high school chemistry teacher from St. Louis, whom I met when Harriet brought her along on one of her subsequent jaunts to Ubud in the 1980s. Harriet's look had evolved a bit — she wore a batik T-shirt and cut-off shorts, and her hair was dyed orange and tied in a ponytail. But our conversation hadn't changed too much over the years — Bali still had "amazing energy" and we still agreed that "it was changing quickly."

One thing that *had* changed was the diversity of spiritual awakening opportunities. I wasn't keeping score, but Harriet was; she availed herself of many of the male-led workshops, all of which seemed to have evocative descriptions. To Harriet it was a compilation of the world's greatest enlightenment menu options: Radiantly Alive and its cousins Surfing the Radiant Life and Alchemy Alive; Breathfest

("Feel more ecstasy, connection and love!"); Blissful Ballroom Dance ("Channel your inner Ginger Rogers!") Seed of Kindness ("Grow your values that correspond with your inner seedlings"); and the musically themed workshops: Tibetan Singing Bowls, Xylophone Vibe Meditation, and several bongo-drum-laden activities.

Then Harriet discovered yoga and began bending into a series of coital postures with mentors in Hatha yoga, Iyengar yoga, Ashtanga yoga, and Bikram yoga. She showed me photos of her sessions at Oxygenated Aerial Yoga, in which she and other participants practiced their *kapotasana* while hanging from bungee cords. She brought her golden retriever Krishna to a workshop titled Yoga with Pets. "That weekend was mind-blowing," she said. "It gave a new meaning to *adho mukha svanasana*." But it was Kundalini yoga that made Harriet aware of ideas that had been floating in her soul but hadn't yet become fully formed – the concept of Tantra and energy lines, power centers and chakras. Her teacher, Ravi Kantowicz, was the "real deal," she said, because he was half-Indian (the other half was Polish, which made for a good combination of auras, her Tarot card reader explained). Besides illuminating her inner beauty, Ravi, whom she met in Kerala, made Harriet aware of the duality of the lingam and yoni. "I've still got an amulet Ravi gave me," she said proudly, pulling out a brass and leather talisman from her bosom. She explained that the phallic-shaped *lingam* on the amulet represents Lord Shiva, god of destruction and creation, while the concave *yoni* is the female feature that represents Shiva's consort Parvati.

The universe needs both Shiva and Parvati to maintain a balance. A system that is all male, or all female, is unhealthy and unsustainable. The two energies complement each other, and together they combine to make life flourish. "It's like the duality of life – sun and moon, day and night, wakefulness and sleep," Harriet explained. "Man and woman. That's what makes the world go round."

I admired her spirit. I admired her ability to continue to seek new frontiers and new challenges to which she would subject her soul and body. But I sensed that she was in a rut, just repeating old patterns.

To my surprise, Harriet agreed. She explained that the dynamics had changed. Her paramours now were gurus first, lovers second. That was an important distinction for Harriet, the realization that the wisdom of wise men could most effectively be conveyed through sex, and that men similarly required a woman's strong female energy to become "complete." In a sense she was doing malekind a favor. She wasn't coy about it; she used graphic terms to describe her metaphysical evolution. She explained her interest in maithuna tantric yoga.

Which led, somehow, I don't recall how, to her ankle bracelet.

I guess I noticed it because I had been admiring her legs. On her left ankle Harriet wore an anklet intricately woven from strands of leather, colored silk threads, and tiny shards of lapis lazuli, turquoise, and peridot. I must have said something mundane like, "That's an interesting piece of jewelry."

She lifted her leg like a ballet dancer and solidly placed her foot onto my lap. "Have a closer look."

I couldn't see anything special.

Harriet laughed. "You see those little hairs woven into the design?"

"The curly ones? They're not ..."

"They are. A little organic souvenir from each of my teachers. I can't have their babies, but I can still carry around a bit of their male energy."

⸻ ••• ⸻

Mind you, not every target teacher succumbed to her charms. I heard through the grapevine that she had convinced a Balinese shaman to let her live in his thatched-roof *lumbung* in the middle of his rice field outside Tamkpaksiring. She paid him well to give her lessons in meditation and Balinese herbalist sorcery. But he gently turned down her offer to spend the *terang bulan* full-moon night with her. Instead, the shaman's teenaged son and two of his friends stopped by with a bottle of Bali rice wine, deciding to try their luck. Harriet at first politely told them she wasn't interested. When they persisted (and Balinese men can be both charming and persistent), she went into a trance she had learned in the Amazon and channeled a snarling jaguar spirit – she growled, exposed her claws, and rolled her eyes back in her head. That did the trick. The youths fled, and her reputation grew.

By the time our paths crossed again in 2010 at the Bali Yoga Festival, Harriet Rabinowitz was experienced enough to make wise life choices, yet still energetic enough to be attractive to many men. (She was now wearing a simple Javanese batik sarong and blue work shirt, and she wore her purple hair very short.)

Harriet needed little prompting to update her story.

Her quests had taken her through the highest ranks of Osho, to the most revered ashrams in the Indian Himalaya, to the Eastern Orthodox monasteries of the Carpathian Mountains. Ages earlier she had "done" the mind-expanding tenets of EST, or Transcendental Meditation. She admitted she had a problem with the Wiccan covens she joined – "Paganism is such a woman's pastime," she complained. "The men in the Wiccan movement either smelled bad or were gay." She was a black belt equivalent in pendulum divination, Native American sweat lodges (an activity run by a shaman who claimed he was a direct descendant of Sitting Bull – Harriet had her doubts, but what the hell), and crystals, and was a whiz at deciphering the softly sung messages of angels. Harriet could meditate with the best of them, bang on a *djembe* so well that she could put herself into a deep trance as quickly as you can say Timothy Leary. Yes, she had imbibed the drugs – opium, mescaline, and ayahuasca, acid and hash (sharing spliffs with near-naked sadhus on the banks of the sacred Ganges at Varanasi). She learned from each experience, even the time she caught gonorrhea from a Tennessee-based pre-Gnostic sage, but she chalked that up to the cost of doing business, like the unavoidable repairs to a car.

A Chinese Taoist master who ran a workshop called Sacred Kung-Fu introduced Harriet to Pangu, considered, in some versions of Chinese mythology, as the creator of the world and the first living being. More important, from Harriet's perspective, is the belief that during Pangu's travails he separated Yin from Yang with a swing of his giant axe. He is often depicted as a primitive, hairy giant. In recognition of Pangu's role in creating female energy that complements male energy, Harriet had a tattoo of the shaggy colossus tattooed on the inside of her left forearm.

Harriet impressed me. She was trying to understand the philosophy that underpinned her "inner drive."

Harriet realized that female "power pilgrims" feature in many religious traditions and spiritual practices. Contrary to Theravada Buddhism as practiced in Thailand, Myanmar, and Sri Lanka, in the Tibetan Nyingma Buddhist tradition, in which Harriet was most interested, being a woman can actually be beneficial for a pilgrim on the path to spiritual realization. Harriet explained the teachings of a Western nun Jetsunma Tenzin Palmo who said that women make superior spiritual practitioners because they are able to "let go" more easily than men. Women have a clarity and an intuitive force that few men possess. At the highest level an enlightened woman might be called a *dakini*; the Sanskrit term means "sky dancer." In a sense a *dakini* is the Eastern equivalent of a Western angel — mysterious and revelatory, a supernatural being who responds to the state of spiritual energy within individuals. Harriet showed me a photo she had torn out of a book. The caption explained it was of a mural in a temple in western Bhutan in which a *dakini* is pictured as a young, naked figure — in one hand she holds the elixir of life and in the other a curved knife. Her hair is unkempt and hangs down her back. She dances wildly on top of a corpse, representing her mastery over ego and ignorance.

To Harriet the sex, or in her jargon "ecstatic enlightenment," was key because it helped her achieve a higher plane of understanding and purity.

To give Harriet due credit, she was a keen student. She not only learned the jargon, which everyone agrees is an important first step, but she also paid attention and became skilled at many of the esoteric trance practices she encountered.

But she was restless. She had climbed so many spiritual mountains that the views, initially glorious, had become mundane. She felt like a food writer who grumbles, "Oh dear, *another* Michelin-starred restaurant tonight."

Something was incomplete in her world, and she was

continually drawn to the Himalaya, the abode of the gods, the home of the most adroit adepts, the supremos of the sadhus, and the greatest of the gurus.

She headed to the Tang Valley of central Bhutan.

And that's where our paths crossed once again.

I was having an espresso in Café Perk, the first and only such establishment in the tiny town of Jakar, in central Bhutan. Most tourists to Bhutan never make it as far east as Jakar. They tend to stay in the western third of the country for two reasons. First, it's relatively expensive to visit Bhutan and those mandatory daily minimum spends can add up. Second, there is only one trunk road running west (where there is an airport) to east (where there isn't), and it is in a state of continual repair, making land journeys long and tedious. But several hundred visitors still make it to Jakar each year. I was there with my wife, who was studying Tibetan Buddhism and writing about a family-owned temple halfway up the Tang Valley, which runs north from Jakar toward the Tibetan border.

Harriet and her sister Freda strode in, wearing new trekking gear – North Face, Patagonia, Quecha, Merrell. "Are the brownies good here?" she asked by way of greeting.

Freda was going to turn around and return to Thimphu the next day. But Harriet explained that she was headed up to the Thowadrak monastery, one of Bhutan's most important monasteries and pilgrimage sites. It was built on a steep mountain a four-hour drive from Jakar up the Tang Valley's only simple road. My wife and I had been there the previous year, and had become friends with Dorje Rigzin, the head abbot, a joyful, gregarious man whose English was limited to "happy," "eat," and "monk."

"And what do you want to do up there?" I asked.

———•••———

The Thowadrak monastery and temple complex is one of the most important pilgrimage sites in Bhutan — Guru Rinpoche, also named Padmasambhava, the saint who brought Tibetan Buddhism to Bhutan, went to Thowadrak in the eighth century to meditate. Along the walk to Thowadrak, the pilgrim passes numerous imprints of Guru Rinpoche's body and feet.

Thowadrak perches on the edge of a cliff, with a shape that resembles a ritual dagger. Bhutanese builders have a skill for constructing houses and temples in dramatic and inaccessible places. One well-known example is the much-visited Paro Taktsang, the Tiger's Nest temple in western Bhutan, which is reachable only via a steep and sometimes vertiginous climb, which is a good example of a structure that defies gravity and inspires the faithful.

When my wife and I climbed up to Thowadrak monastery, it quickly became apparent that she was in better shape than I was; it took me a wheezy two hours to reach the monastery perched on a promontory at around four thousand meters. The abbot knew we were coming (cell phone service is surprisingly good in rural Bhutan) and had instructed the apprentice monks to blow their trumpets in welcome when they saw us approaching. This they did, while we were some one hundred meters below the building. It reminded me of a Monty Python-type film, in which the monks played a fanfare indicating "the honored guests are arriving." When we hadn't arrived after ten minutes, they blew their trumpets again, no doubt announcing "the honored guests are still approaching." Ten minutes later, as we slowly continued our climb, the trumpets sounded again and the monks no doubt intoned "the honored guests are almost amongst us." By the time we finally arrived, panting and heady from the altitude, the monk-trumpet welcoming committee had given up and gone to lunch.

So I told Harriet that the monastery was difficult to reach, that no one there spoke English, and that the meditation caves were hidden much farther up the mountain. "Anyway, I doubt the abbot will let you anywhere near the caves. They're only for serious monks."

She smiled at the idea of this new adventure. "No pain, no gain," she said, rather unoriginally, and added, "Victory often comes to the breathless."

We chatted for a while, and as my wife and I were getting ready to leave Harriet asked, "What do you know about the *terton* up in Thowadrak?"

A *terton*? Why was she asking about a treasure revealer? Harriet surprised me.

I would have thought she would inquire about a different monk in Thowadrak who was said to be an incarnation of Drupka Kunley, who seemed like her ideal ecstatic enlightenment mentor.

Throughout Bhutan a visitor is intrigued to see phalluses prominently painted on many homes in the country. Dasho Karma Ura, of the Center for Bhutan Studies, describes these large and anatomically correct images, called *po* in Dzonghka, Bhutan's national language, as "exuberant and gifted penises, always slightly askew and sometimes frothy." They protect families from evil spirits and the pervasive threats of slander and gossip.

The man who generally gets credited with popularizing this good-luck-phallus belief was a fifteenth- to sixteenth-century Buddhist lama named Drukpa Kunley. He was to phallus admiration what Brigitte Bardot was to the bikini.

Unlike the gentle and placid approach of mainstream Buddhist missionaries, Drukpa Kunley proselytized through anarchy, shock, and awe. He believed that only by spotlighting the absurdity of all fixed, man-made rules, and by forcing the student to abandon all ideas of predictability and emotional security, can people become wise enough to understand the "crazy wisdom" of Buddhist enlightenment.

Drukpa Kunley, *enfant terrible* of Buddhist missionaries, seducer of women (including his own mother, but it was for her own good, he argued), famously subdued the female demons of Bhutan with his "Thunderbolt of Flaming Wisdom." He exemplified the tantric belief that carnal relations can be the gateway to enlightenment, and he was not hesitant to enlighten as many women as possible. He was called "The Saint of 5,000 Women."

It is said that Drukpa Kunley, one of the few Buddhist teachers to almost always appear in Bhutanese paintings topless, would not bless any man who came to seek his guidance unless he brought a beautiful woman and a bottle of wine.

Harriet said that Drukpa Kunley would have been interesting for her some years earlier, but she had reached the stage of her spiritual journey that she was ready for more than flaming thunderbolts.

Yes, I told her, there were stories that one of the meditating monks at Thowadrak was a possible *terton*, a powerful young saint who is able to find *terma*, the Tibetan term for sacred religious artifacts and teachings that had been hidden by ancient sages. These spiritual treasures might take the form of statues, sacred texts, songs, or philosophical insights. One famous *terma* familiar to lay Westerners is the religious text *Bardo Thodol*, popularly known as the *Tibetan Book of the Dead*.

My wife explained to Harriet why the Tang Valley is one of the epicenters of Bhutanese *terton/terma* activity.

In the fourteenth century, the Tibetan lama Dorje Lingpa visited the family-owned manor estate and temple of Ogyen Choling, halfway up the Tang Valley. Dorje Lingpa is one of the five Sovereign *tertons*, the most gifted treasure revealers among the one hundred major *tertons* and more than a thousand minor *tertons* recorded from Tibet and Bhutan.

And the most important Bhutanese *terton*, Pema Lingpa (also one of the five Sovereign, or superstar, *tertons*), was born in the Tang Valley in the fifteenth century. Pema Lingpa, who was a disciple of Guru Rinpoche, is also revered as an ancestor of the current Bhutanese royal family.

Pema Lingpa discovered his first *terma* in a deep pool at a dramatic narrow gorge on the Tang River, at the lower end of the Tang Valley, just outside the town of Jakar. The chronicles of Pema Lingpa's life report that in 1475 he followed specific instructions given to him by a divine messenger and went to the river's edge. Suddenly he found himself in a large underwater cavern where a one-eyed deity gave him an ornate box and a parchment scroll. When Pema Lingpa recovered from the trance on the bank of the river, he was holding the box and scroll. The scroll (which might have been as small as a slip of paper) was said to be written in the arcane *dayig* script, a metaphysical construct that one researcher suggested might be equated with the hidden language of Atlantis. Harriet was delighted to learn that *dayig* writing is also termed *dakini*, named after the celestial *dakinis* that so entranced Harriet. On a subsequent visit to convince skeptics of his ability, Pema Lingpa dove into the same deep pool holding a burning butter lamp. He surfaced triumphantly, brandishing ritual skulls and a statue. His butter lamp was still burning, hence the designation of the site as Mebartsho, the Burning Lake.

Harriet added she had heard that male tertons are often energized by the complementary dynamism of female consorts with whom they practice sexual yoga, or *karmamudra*, to accelerate and enhance their capacity for realization.

And even more interesting for Harriet was the belief that women can also become *tertons*.

———•••———

I thought that this would be the end of Harriet's Bhutan adventure. Surely the abbot would be polite and let her spend the night in the monastery and then send her on her way. And there was the question of her guide. Unaccompanied tourists are discouraged in Bhutan, especially folks who want to visit a holy site not far from the Tibetan border that requires an arduous climb to reach.

But I underestimated Harriet's determination. As Freda recounted some months later, via email and Skype, Harriet told her guide, Sonam Tsering, that she was going to spend some time hanging around Jakar and that he should escort her sister Freda back to the airport in Paro from where she was scheduled to fly on to Bangkok. Sonam booked Harriet into a Jakar guest house. "Come back and get me in ten days," Harriet told him.

Reluctantly, Sonam agreed. As soon as he was out of sight, Harriet went to the market and arranged to hitch a ride on a potato truck headed up the Tang Valley. Never mind that she was putting Sonam's career in jeopardy. She was always selfish; I think it's a condition of pilgrimhood.

Then the story gets murky. Our hosts at the temple, who were in regular contact with the abbot, filled us in on Harriet's exploits.

———•••———

Harriet arrived at the temple late one rainy afternoon, wearing a heavy backpack and carrying a heart full of anticipation. Apparently the abbot understood more English than I had given him credit for, and Harriet was able to make her desires known.

"Impossible," the abbot replied, but no doubt phrasing it in a subtle Bhutanese manner. He offered her dinner, showed her where the toilets were, and left her alone while he went about his evening prayers.

Harriet hung around Thowadrak for a couple of days, getting acclimatized to the altitude and making friends with the dozen or so young monks and the wife and children of the abbot, who also lived in the temple complex. She surprised them by knowing some of the prayers and rituals that make the Bhutanese form of Tibetan Buddhism so rich and vibrant.

One night, around midnight, Harriet walked behind the temple to a gorge behind a ridge, called the "Water of Nine As." Here, it is said, one hundred thousand *dakinis* bathed Guru Rinpoche. Harriet tranced and danced like a wild *dakini*. Naked, she waved a skull in one hand and a trident in the other, both holy relics borrowed from the monastery's chapel. Harriet wailed a dirge that echoed through the valley. It could have been "Oh What a Beautiful Morning" from *Oklahoma* executed in a minor key and performed in a guttural voice and glacial tempo. It might have been the Kyrie from Berlioz's *Requiem*. It could have been a dark celestial performance of Harriet's orgasm.

Two witnesses said they saw her levitate.

Her atonal howling lasted some twenty minutes, by which time every resident of the monastery had come to witness the event. When Harriet finally collapsed in exhaustion, all members of her audience stood in silent prayer for a moment before ministering to the woman, wrapping her in blankets and carrying her back to the monastery.

The abbot agreed to allow Harriet to spend three days in a meditation cave. He had told me on our earlier visit that the cave experience was reserved for serious monks who had already spent years meditating and enduring deprivations. These were the monks who were learning teleportation and how to control their body temperature to survive naked in a cave at more than four thousand meters during a Bhutanese winter. They could live on love and fresh air.

The abbot got Harriet settled in at a damp, small hollow, which the monks had dubbed "the foreign woman's cave." It was the same fissure where Gelongma Lama Palmo had meditated several decades earlier. Gelongma Palmo (née Sabine Januschkel in 1970) from Vienna, was one of the very few female lamas of Buddhism and the first non-Asian, female Choje Lama in the twenty-six-hundred-year-old history of Buddhism. The abbot promised Harriet he would return the next morning with some rice.

***

Now comes the speculation.

Harriet did a bit of meditation (she could only sit in *padmasana* for half an hour, max) and then got restless. She wandered across the ridge to a neighboring cave, some three hundred meters distant. While approaching the cave mouth she came across a skinny, bearded monk wearing a surprisingly clean monk's robe. From information she had gleaned at the monastery, she recognized him as Jigme Dorje, the *terton*.

Jigme Dorje was returning from the forest nearby, where he had answered the call of nature. One can imagine his surprise. He was polite and invited Harriet to share a glass of cold spring water. Harriet apparently said the right things, proved her fidelity to the precepts of Lord Buddha, and invited herself to share Jigme Dorje's cave.

During the night the monk shook the snoring Harriet awake. (Her snore, it was said, could frighten a yak and stop the sun from rising.) Harriet emitted a satisfied *hmmm, more enlightenment.*

But Jigme Dorje simply put his finger to his lips, indicating she should shut up, pointed to the darkness outside the cave, and whispered *migoi.*

They quietly moved to the mouth of the cave and sat quietly. After perhaps half an hour, a full-moon-generated human-like shadow appeared, accompanied by a noxious stench. Imagine. A short, skinny near-naked Bhutanese monk, and a slightly fluffier near-naked American Harriet, one comfortable enfolded in a full lotus, the other sitting on a rock and shivering in the cold, looking up at the most special of Lord Buddha's creations. It was a *migoi*, the Bhutanese version of the yeti.

The Tang Valley is a prime habitat for the creatures. I had gone on my own *migoi*-seeking expedition some years earlier, but that's another story.

According to our hosts at the family-owned temple, who heard it from the abbot, who heard it from the monk, the *migoi* sat down and began to eat the scraps of rice that remained from the monk's meal the previous day. The *migoi* smelled terrible, farted, and belched, but he wasn't aggressive. It was almost as if he accepted these human visitors in his mountain domain.

And then the *migoi* stood up, calmly swept Harriet into his arms, and strolled away. According to our hosts, who heard it from the abbot, who heard it from the monk, Harriet did not scream or protest. The monk couldn't be sure, but he thought that as Harriet and the *migoi* disappeared into the shadows, she gave him a Thai *wai*, a symbol of peace that meant "May god go with you."

The monk had no doubt that the *migoi* was a *terma*, a treasure that, if properly decoded, would provide important insights into the veneration of Lord Buddha.

Eventually, somehow, Harriet escaped her cryptoid hominoid kidnapper and made her way back to Jakar. She was waiting peacefully for Sonam when he returned to Jakar on schedule to escort her back to Paro where she would board her flight to Bangkok.

Meanwhile, the monk Jigme Dorje confessed his inappropriate behavior to the abbot. Jigme Dorje was removed from his cave and given a sentence of one year's work chopping wood, cleaning the temple grounds, emptying the toilets, and peeling onions. But word of his *migoi* encounter somehow spread throughout the valley, and his reputation as a great *terton* was established.

The abbot, perhaps seeking a bit of the *terton* limelight himself, took to spending full-moon nights in one of the vacant meditation caves. It is not known whether he had his own *migoi* encounter.

The guide Sonam asked Harriet what she had done while he was gone. "Oh, just wandered around some monasteries and talked to people. Soaked up the local culture." He accepted her superficial answer.

Harriet refused to talk about her experience. But she has two new additions to her ankle bracelet.

Epilogue

Dinanukht Lounges Around
Reading Himself

Inspiration for our age or phony prophet?

TANAH LOT
Bali, Indonesia

"Dinanukht sits on a rock between the waters of the world, reading himself. At least that's how the story goes," I said. My friend Ariel and I were sitting on a cliff overlooking a seaside Balinese temple and I wanted to see if she could help me in yet another of my pointless quests.

"I want to speak with Dinanukht," I said. "Get the story from the horse's mouth, as it were."

"Hmmm," she said.

"Is that a good 'hmmm' or a bad 'hmmm'?"

"Neutral." She threw the question back at me, a trick loved by psychiatrists and journalists. And, in her case, a ploy favored by psychic mediums. "And what's *your* version?"

"Haven't decided yet. I was hoping you would help."

"Hmmm," she said again. Her "hmmms" get irritating after a while. Then she got excited. "Interesting conundrum. If a person could read herself, would that mean she also had the ability to write herself? Is her story internalized or universal? Frippery or intensity?"

"Exactly," I said. "But I needed to keep Ariel grounded. But don't forget the basics: What did Dinanukht read? And did he write the text himself?"

Ariel Maya Berimpi, a "wise woman" of Balinese, Irish, and Aztec ancestry, paused for a moment. She gazed out toward the temple of Tanah Lot, which sits on a partially submerged spit of land just off the southwest coast of Bali. "Let me ask him."

And, quicker than you could say Arthur Schopenhauer, Ariel was off into one of her trances, summoning her "ancestor guide" who would assist her in contacting Dinanukht. Ariel mumbled an ancient Sanskrit mantra to go into her altered state.

While waiting for her to enter the "in-between world" as she called it, I too pondered the question of what Dinanukht read. The only answer I could come up with was that hoary cop-out: It depends. What reading matter would an ancient god from a virtually extinct Middle Eastern Gnostic sect have on his bedside table? Probably would depend on his mood, I decided. *Mad* magazine. *À la recherche du temps perdu.* The ingredients list on a box of corn flakes. The *Epic of Gilgamesh.* Shakespeare's sonnets. Montaigne's essays. This morning's sports pages. A biography of Calvin Coolidge. All the Louis L'Amour westerns. The *Foundation* trilogy. Catherine the Great's personal journal. Cleopatra's memos to her chamberlain complaining about the quality of the olive oil. The legal disclaimer on Ian Fleming's bus pass.

Suddenly, Ariel's body shook and her posture became stiff and puppet-like.

"You ask an impertinent question, Mister Paul." It was Ariel's voice but spoken from a deep, almost masculine register. Her normal Pan-Asian accent had been replaced by a stronger, lower-register brogue, almost guttural. Her pronunciation was deliberate. Her eyes wouldn't focus on me.

"Top of the morning, Dinanukht," I said.

Ariel's face twitched.

Even though Dinanukht had been sidelined for two thousand years and was a tiny footnote in a giant tome of neglected gods and mythological heroes, perhaps I was overstepping the fundamentals of basic respect. But I give little deference for the deities that people have created to guarantee safe passage to a jolly afterworld.

"Harumph," he said through Ariel, whose hands were supplicating the sky for reasons unknown. Was that a Persian twang I heard?"

"Dinanukht," I said. "I don't speak ancient Aramaic. Nor Persian. Nor Arabic. Not Hebrew either, or Syriac."

"Seems like you don't speak much of anything. How can we have a sensible dialogue?"

"How about English. Or Indonesian?"

Dinanukht/Ariel made his grumpy sound.

"French?"

"I'm too busy to waste time with you," Dinanukht/Ariel said. "Why did you take me away from my rock between the waters?"

Then he continued, through Ariel, in refined British English like a character out of Trollope. "Why are you talking instead of reading, like civilized people do?"

"I read. But more importantly I write," I said, angry that he scolded me.

"A tepid response," said Dinanukht/Ariel. "Next you'll blabber, 'I slink, therefore I scam.'"

Change course. Maybe I was too aggressive. "Dinanukht, listen. Is it okay if I call you Dinanukht? Or should it be Lord Dinanukht? Or Your Holy Eminence Dinanukht?"

"It makes little difference." Then an afterthought: "Sage Dinanukht would be acceptable."

"So, Sage Dinanukht," I said. "I have two questions for you."

"You want to know your fate? When you'll ascend to the Light World? How boring."

"No, I don't give a damn about my fate. But I'm curious about what it is you read all day, sitting between the waters of the world."

His voice changed to that of a street urchin out of *Les Miserables*. "You are so literal, silly man. You think that because my body is full of words that I myself am a book."

"That's what the legends say."

"Legends schmegends," he said laughing. His voice now sounded like an F. Scott Fitzgerald character. "I read because I am more amusing than anything ever written by Aristophanes, more profound than anything written by Krishnamurti, more thought-provoking than Siddhartha, more sentimental than Hallmark, more hummable than a Disney song, more moralistic than Dante, more inspirational than Genghis Khan's battle cry before he invaded Poland...."

"You just made that last bit up."

"I'm a writer. I can make up anything I like. And if you don't like it, then bugger off."

Was that Oscar Wilde? "*Bugger off*? That's no way for a god to talk."

"You should hear it when Odin, Shiva, Osiris, and I get together for a bowl of ambrosia. Sometimes Artemis joins in. That woman, raised by wolves, I think. She's got a mouth on her."

I didn't want Robin Williams sounding like a Jewish mother butting in right now. "You're ... you're just derivative," I said. A weak riposte, I know.

I am the very model of a modern gnostic deity
I assimilate great books from the library of posterity

With Ruha's help I encourage pre-Christian charity
I sit and read the papers with great artistic ability
And guard my legacy from every scheming wannabe.

"Derivative," I said again.

And Dinanukht/Ariel went silent. Perhaps I had overstepped my role as a supplicant. I guess I should have eased up on him. The poor guy was trying to write memorable literature using an obscure variant of a virtually forgotten descendant language of Phoenician and distant cousin to Modern Hebrew. Each letter has magical implications. No wonder Dinanukht sounded a bit spacey.

Plus, he's no ordinary deity. Not quite a god, more of a metaphor. He was the wisest of the twenty-four Wise Men, who were wise indeed. Sacred books revealing The Way kept on appearing to him; he read each one and they led him on his journey to the World of Light. The writing on his body, some scholars say, is a *Da Vinci Code*-like cipher, accessible only to Mandaean priests, offering inspiration and tactical guidance to enable believers to follow the Light. A scribe? A saint? A teaching tool? Who was this snarky character with whom I was chatting?

"I was expecting something more profound," I said, trying to be friendly. "Maybe some Rumi."

Dinanukht/Ariel then chanted, while Ariel waved her arms as if she was at a rock concert:

As I explained this morning to Rumi
It's all very well to whirl a Sufi

The troubadours sing loud your Mathnawi
And struggle to recall your Masnavi
People read and wish to soar with angels
No death does ever fear your soppy culls
Your doggerel no death does ever fear
For me I'd rather have another beer.

"Hold on," I said. "Don't go bashing Rumi. He's terrific. Deep, sensitive, opening new doors of consciousness ..."

"A loathsome prig, a low-life pretending to be well-bred, unworthy to share a table with the gentlefolk." A Russian accent. Tolstoy?

"Is not."

"Is too."

"And never mind Rumi, your verse doesn't even scan properly," I yelled. "Hah. You call yourself a poet."

"More than you'll ever be," Dinanukht/Ariel countered.

"It's not so hard – it's a simple Noel Coward rip-off structure, ten syllables and a childish rhyme AA-BB-CC-DD."

"Not my fault. No connection here, couldn't access the rhyming dictionary." With that statement Dinanukht/Ariel tapped her stomach as if looking for a USB port.

"You have Wi-Fi in that Teletubby body?"

"You don't expect me to carry around heavy books, do you?"

"I'm disappointed. I thought you were self-contained, that you wrote all your own stuff."

"When I have the energy. I'm two thousand years old you know."

"Just as I thought. You haven't had a book out in two millennia," I scolded. It was my turn to "harumph" in disdain. "Who listens to a god who doesn't publish? You might lose tenure. No wonder nobody believes in you anymore."

"A proud god will live forever in the hearts of wise men."

Sounded like Homer. Maybe Virgil. Either way I wasn't getting anywhere by arguing with him. Try to be conciliatory. "But you read yourself. Every legend says the same thing. Seriously, do you write your own material?"

"Can't you read?" he said. "My body is covered with symbols, full of enlightening clues if one is able to decipher them."

Agatha Christie? No, it couldn't be. I examined the cuneiform-like symbols on his head and torso. "You've got to get with the times. Aramaic stopped being a literary language back when Sheba was queen."

"Hah, what do you know about connecting with readers. Besides, I'm the only reader who counts."

"Just tell me – what does your body say?"

Ariel was getting tired, and perhaps Dinanukht was also losing patience. The tide was going out and tourists were starting to wade across the shallows to Tanah Lot. I could hear them shouting as if they were at a theme park, not one of Bali's holiest sites.

"My head is the weather report," Dinanukht/Ariel said. "Here in Bali it's boringly monotonous. Every day around thirty degrees, high humidity, some sun mixed with some rain. Good for growing orchids and mangoes. Useless for doing sustained labor."

"And your body?"

"That, my unenlightened cynical friend, is the key to my existence. My body is my existence. The only reality is duality, and the quicker you realize that the easier you'll sleep at night. Black and white, male and female, yin and yang, night and day, rainy season and dry season, good and bad, fire and water, truth and lie, acid and alkaline, greed and generosity. Must I continue?"

"It was the best of times, it was the worst of times," I said sarcastically.

"That's good, mind if I borrow it?"

"Go ahead, Dickens is dead anyway. But why this fascination with opposites?"

"We can only define reality by what it is not. Just as I was telling Disai, that scheming interloper. Hah! He thought he was a better book than I was. You know he tried to prevent me from escorting souls to the Light of the World. Ah, I can tell you're not interested."

"And there is *one* book that contains all these things?" I was thinking of the *Mahabharata* perhaps, or *The Iliad*.

"There is one book that *is* all-enlightening. *Chronicles of a Static Wanderer*," Dinanukht/Ariel said.

"Never heard of it. An old Mayan text?"

"Ignorant puppy. It's mine. Sixteen thousand, eight hundred fifty-four pages of genius. Single-spaced. Rejected by thousands of publishers. Idiots."

That was the first thing he said that resonated. So I asked, "Have you read anything of mine?"

"Who are you again?"

So I explained who I was, why I was in Bali (to attend a joint United Nations-ASEAN conference on a community income-generating project to transform rice husks into costume jewelry). And I told him about my books, how they are filled with encounters with exceptional people who had something to teach me, people with wisdom to share and messages of cynicism and hope, greed and generosity, dreams and ambitions.

"Never heard of you."

"I'm on Kindle," I said defensively.

"Are you going to write about me?"

"Depends if you ever say anything memorable." Then I changed tack. "And what are you working on now?"

"Something that will change the way of the world. It's the answer to the question, 'What is the secret of the universe?' and it's not the number forty-two. Amazingly, it all fits into a five-seven-five haiku. Want to hear it?"

Before I could say yes, I saw that Ariel was twitching and rolling on the ground. She had lost contact with Dinanukht. It was starting to rain. I gave her a chance to "return" to our perch on the clifftop in Bali.

"Do you remember what happened?" I asked her moments later.

"No."

So I told her what had taken place.

"Dinanukht's never been so loquacious before. He must have liked you," she said.

We started walking back to a nearby restaurant to seek shelter and get some lunch.

"Funny, I have a haiku in my head," Ariel said once we were settled and somewhat dried off. "Don't know what it means."

"Quick, tell me."

And she did.

Give me a big D/
Create and never forget/
Rose by other name

Time is running out for the people and the orangutans who share this threatened environment. Who has the answer to saving the world's oldest forest — the marketing experts of an international nature conservation group or the earnest monkey-wrenchers?

"Redheads does for the struggle to save the rain forests of Borneo what *Catch*-22 did for the struggle to stay alive in World War II."

—Daniel Quinn, author of *Ishmael*

"Free-thinking, intelligent and irreverent — *Redheads* reminds me of a Kurt Vonnegut thriller. It's bold, pacey — even racy — a quirky and often laugh-out-loud funny Robin Hood parable about the willful destruction of Asia's forests and the price we pay by turning a blind eye. I loved this visceral eco-thriller, a sort of jungle morality-play in which there's more than simply the trees to lose."

—Benedict Allen, author of *Hunting the Gugu: In Search of the Lost Ape-Men of Sumatra*

AN INORDINATE FONDNESS FOR BEETLES

CAMPFIRE CONVERSATIONS WITH ALFRED RUSSEL WALLACE ON PEOPLE AND NATURE BASED ON COMMON TRAVEL IN THE MALAY ARCHIPELAGO, THE LAND OF THE ORANGUTAN, AND THE BIRD OF PARADISE

Explorer's Eye Press. Geneva. 2017.
ISBN: 978-2-940573-25-7

An Inordinate Fondness for Beetles follows the Victorian-era explorations of Alfred Russel Wallace through Southeast Asia. While Wallace is recognized as co-discoverer of the theory of natural selection (and was perhaps deliberately sidelined by Darwin), he was also an edgy social commentator and a voracious collector of "natural productions."

In this innovative form of storytelling, combining incisive biography and personal travelogue, Sochaczewski examines themes about which Wallace cared deeply and interprets them through his own filter with layers of humor, history, social commentary, and sometimes outrageous personal tales.

❖

"A new category of nonfiction – part personal travelogue, part incisive biography, part unexpected traveler's tales."
—Jeffrey Sayer, professor of conservation and development at James Cook University

"Reading *Beetles* was as if I had boarded a time machine to accompany Wallace ... a revelation of Wallace's mesmerizing natural history insights interwoven with Sochaczewski's unique view of the world and our place in it."
—Thomas E. Lovejoy, professor at George Mason University, senior fellow at the United Nations Foundation

"The rhythm and magic of a verbal fugue."
—Dato Sri Gathorne, author of *Mammals of Borneo*

"A fascinating journey ... Thought-provoking about change and constancy, and a delight to read."
—Peter H. Raven, president emeritus of the Missouri Botanical Garden

SHARE YOUR JOURNEY
MASTERING PERSONAL WRITING

Explorer's Eye Press. Geneva. 2016.
ISBN: 978-2-940573-15-8

Share Your Journey is an easy-to-use handbook for people who want to write their personal stories but aren't sure how to start and how to make them interesting. It's based on the writing workshops I've run in more than twenty countries. The book provides ten techniques professional authors use to write memoirs and travel stories that connect with readers and editors.

"This is a lifetime's wisdom, offered by a pro. Put it next to *The Elements of Style* by Strunk and White – they'll be the only two writing books you'll need."

—Thomas Bass, author of *The Spy Who Loved Us*

"*Share Your Journey* is to good writing as *Joy of Cooking* is to good food. I wish all my students had this book before taking my writing classes. Hell, I wish I had this book earlier in my career. It's smart, fun, and every page contains nuggets of essential advice."
—Gary Goshgarian, professor of creative writing, Northeastern University

"Paul Sochaczewski offers ten simple, but too often overlooked guidelines, then amply (and memorably) illustrates how easily it can be done."
—Jerry Hopkins, former editor of *Rolling Stone*, author of *No One Here Gets Out Alive*

"Many writing guides turn what should be a liberating experience into drudgery and scolding rules. *Share Your Journey* is different; it helps you unleash an inner voice you may not have realized was inside you. It's also great fun."
—Nigel Barley, author of *Island of Dreams*

"Like all serious writers, Sochaczewski has no hesitation mixing the wit with the chaff. This book is caviar for those who long to express themselves."
—Harry Rolnick, author of *The Complete Book of Coffee*

"The memorable tool kit Sochaczewski presents allows a writer with a story and some raw talent to build a word castle that rises to the heavens."
—Christopher G. Moore, author of the Vincent Calvino novels

CURIOUS ENCOUNTERS OF THE HUMAN KIND

TRUE ASIAN TALES OF FOLLY, GREED, AMBITION, AND DREAMS

Explorer's Eye Press. Geneva. 2016.

A five volume series – Myanmar (Burma), Southeast Asia, Indonesia, Himalaya, and Borneo – containing true stories based on Sochaczewski's forty-five years of living and exploring in curious corners of Asia. This is Asia as you've probably never imagined, full of memorable people, startling happenings, and unexpected moments of humanity and introspection, giddiness and solemnity, avarice and ambition.

Some highlights: How do "often frothy" phalluses protect Bhutanese villagers? Does the yeti illuminate the dark side of our souls? What is the allure of Waltzing Banana Island? How does a Papuan hunter juggle the four religions that want a piece of his soul? What is the attraction of coffee that's been digested by a civet? How has a town named after a female vampire ghost spawned an entire genre of kitschy horror films? Can two-hundred-million-year-old fossilized shark dung bring you good luck?

"The spirit of Kipling in contemporary Asian journalism. This collection is essential reading for anyone who wishes to pass beyond even the unbeaten track, right to the heart of Asia."

—John Burdett, author of *Bangkok Asset*

"The humanity of Somerset Maugham, the adventure of Joseph Conrad, the perception of Paul Theroux, and a self-effacing voice uniquely his own."

—Gary Braver, bestselling author of *Skin Deep*

"A fun, and funny, introduction to South and Southeast Asia. A must-read for all serious travelers."

—Jonah Blank, author of *Arrow of the Blue-Skinned God: Retracing the Ramayana Through India*

"Pellucid writing, insightful irreverence, and universal truths elegantly presented, in a genre that defies categorization."

—John Keay, author of *When Men and Mountains Meet* and *India: A History*

DISTANT GREENS
GOLF, LIFE, AND SURPRISING SERENDIPITY ON AND OFF THE FAIRWAYS

Explorer's Eye Press. Geneva. 2016.
ISBN: 978-2-940573-21-9

Distant Greens travels to the highest golf course in the world, where breathless Tibetan precepts come face to face with the Indian military. To a golf course in the Amazon rainforest, near the source of rubber, which revolutionized the game. To the Middle Kingdom, to examine claims that it was the Chinese who invented golf. And to a volcanic Indonesian course where the Mermaid Queen ensures that "her" sultan always has good weather when he plays.

Distant Greens examines the future of golf and shows that a well-designed, well-managed golf course can protect nature.

Distant Greens also travels into the soul of golf. Why do people cheat? Why do golfers remember the bad shots instead of the good shots? And why is golf more important, to some folks, than sex?

"An intimate golfing tour that travels to all corners of the planet and brings us into the heart, mind, and soul of the game that we all love."

—Rick Lipsey, *Sports Illustrated*

"*Distant Greens* get to the core of golf's eco-spiritual essence with a collection of charming, penetrating stories and commentary that traverse the globe yet reside happily in the realm of 'good heart.'"

—Steve Cohen, president, The Shivas Irons Society

"Insightful essays and exceptional reportage explore new vistas and get to the heart of the very reason so many of us love this game."

—Fred Shoemaker, founder of Extraordinary Golf

SOUL OF THE TIGER
SEARCHING FOR NATURE'S ANSWERS IN
SOUTHEAST ASIA

Jeffrey A. McNeely and Paul Spencer Sochaczewski
University of Hawai'i Press. Honolulu. 1995.
ISBN 0-82481-669-2

Soul of the Tiger takes us to an increasingly threatened world where human life is intimately linked with rhinos and cobras, elephants and man-eating tigers — both in the physical world as well as the metaphysical and divine realms. To people in Southeast Asia animals are omens, divinities, meat, leather, competitors, and sometimes ancestors.

Soul of the Tiger identifies the four "eco-cultural revolutions" that have permanently and dramatically changed the face of Southeast Asia. And the authors suggest a fifth "eco-cultural revolution," which could lead to a new sustainable relationship between people and nature.

First published in 1988, *Soul of the Tiger* (which has never been out of print) has become a classic in the literature of modern conservation. As one recent reviewer noted: "Age has not diminished the value of this book; it remains a classic in the genres of both conservation and travel literature."

⸺•••⸺

"A timely, revealing, delightful and yet totally unsentimental look at the relationship between our own and other species, which must lie at the heart of all successful conservation."
—Lyall Watson, author of *Supernature*

"A marvelous book, unique, intelligent, attuned to cultures and filled with stimulating ideas."
—George Schaller, director of Wildlife Conservation International

"One fascinating account after another. The authors conclude that traditional human-wildlife relations should be encouraged in a world that seeks to balance economic growth and environmental preservation."
—John Noble Wilford in *The New York Times*

ECO BLUFF YOUR WAY TO GREENISM
The Guide to Instant Environmental Credibility

Paul Sochaczewski (in this book writing as Paul Wachtel)
and Jeffrey A. McNeely
Bonus Books. Chicago. 1991.
ISBN 0-929387-22-8

Eco-Bluff Your Way to Greenism provides instruction on how to attain quick and painless eco-credibility, giving essential advice on such things as how to deal with people who prefer elephants to human beings, how to establish your street-cred by explaining the public relations coup of Chief Seattle (use his real name Seathl to further impress your friends), and how to stir up a party by roaring like an eco-guerilla.

"What a book! Covers insights into potentially disastrous global issues in a bright and (dare I say) enjoyable way. Takes no prisoners and opens our eyes to a new and more effective vision of the pathway to environmental sanity."
—Noel Vietmeyer, US National Academy of Sciences

"A hilarious romp through the lexicon of eco-babble, replete with telling jabs at the people, institutions, and jargon of the Green world.... Powerfully signals the sweeping breadth of the authors' knowledge about environmental affairs. Learn while you laugh."
—Roger D. Stone, author *Dreams of Amazonia*

THE SULTAN AND THE MERMAID QUEEN
SURPRISING ASIAN PEOPLE, PLACES, AND THINGS THAT GO BUMP IN THE NIGHT

Editions Didier Millet. Singapore. 2008.
ISBN 978-981-4217-74-3

The Sultan and the Mermaid Queen is a collection of seventy essays and articles that describe seldom written about Asian people, places, and events.

You'll learn why Javanese sultans owe their power to the Mermaid Queen. Ponder why isolated Indian villagers are angry at the Monkey God Hanuman for not returning their sacred mountain. Learn why the Indonesian island of Flores is ground-zero for "small people" fables and reality. And understand why the ninety-year-old "last elephant hunter" of Vietnam was offered a lucrative product endorsement for a virility tonic.

"Sochaczewski is a world-class searcher, reporter, and observer who has crisscrossed Asia for forty years, pausing in the most unlikely places, finding extraordinary people, and along the way has gathered and shaped an insightful, witty chronicle. His essays are filled with a rich tapestry of wannabe royalty, curious naturalists, Hindu gods, and Buddhist monks. He is a knowledgeable guide to an often obscure world."

—Christopher G. Moore,
author of *Heart Talk*

"The humanity of Somerset Maugham, the adventure of Joseph Conrad, the perception of Paul Theroux, and a self-effacing voice uniquely his own."

—Gary Braver, author of *Skin Deep*

"Each true story is a gem constructed with a fine touch and disarming insight. On one level, the stories tell of Paul's personal quests, but he has achieved something extraordinary, something all writers could emulate. To his core reporting he adds layers: a touch of history, a sprinkle of mythology, an insight of philosophy, a handful of (relevant) trivia, a large grain of post-modernist thinking, even a smidgen of geopolitics. The result is like a series of curries in which the ingredients add up to more than the sum of its parts – rich, satisfying, spicy, otherworldly."

—James Clad, former US deputy assistant secretary of
defense for Asia Pacific

About the Author

Paul in Borneo, researching "Slouching Toward Bethlehem."

Paul Spencer Sochaczewski is a Geneva-based writer and writing coach. While with WWF (World Wide Fund for Nature International), Paul created global campaigns to protect rainforests and biological diversity, and then developed the WWF Faith and Environment program.

Paul has lived and worked in more than eighty countries, including two decades in Southeast Asia. He has written more than six hundred by-lined articles for *The New York Times*, *The International Herald Tribune*, *Wall Street Journal*, *Travel and Leisure*, *CNN Traveller*, *Reader's Digest*, and *Geographical*. In addition, he has written about the nature of Malaysia in *Malaysia: Heart of Southeast Asia*, served on the Editorial Advisory Board for the *Indonesian Heritage Encyclopedia*, and was project initiator for *Tanah Air: Celebrating Indonesia's Biodiversity*.

And because this is a book of fantasy, Paul is a daring giant-wave surfer (four-time winner of the Quiksilver in Memory of Eddie Aikau on Oahu's North Shore), has summited K2 without supplemental oxygen, proven that *orang pendek*, which he dubbed "snowmen of the jungle," live in the rainforests of Sumatra (he spent three weeks with a troupe of the elusive hominoids, whose existence had never been proven, recording their vocalizations and filming their daily activities), studied teleportation techniques with a Bhutanese Tantra master, and has won three Pulitzer Prizes for his incisive writing and commentary. He has never spoken publicly about his arm-wrestling victory over Arnold Schwarzenegger. George Clooney or Harrison Ford will star in a biopic of Paul's life, now in pre-production.

www.sochaczewski.com

www.ingramcontent.com/pod-product-compliance
Lightning Source LLC
Chambersburg PA
CBHW020023310726
48970CB00007B/2183